Maz Evans

VI SPY

THE GIRL WITH THE GOLDEN GRAN

Chicken House

2 Palmer Street, Frome, Somerset BA11 1DS
www.chickenhousebooks.com

Text © Mary Evans 2022
Illustrations © Jez Tuya 2022

First published in Great Britain in 2022
Chicken House
2 Palmer Street
Frome, Somerset BA11 1DS
United Kingdom
www.chickenhousebooks.com

Chicken House/Scholastic Ireland, 89E Lagan Road, Dublin Industrial Estate,
Glasnevin, Dublin D11 HP5F, Republic of Ireland

Cover and interior design by Steve Wells and Helen Crawford-White
Cover and interior illustrations by Jez Tuya
Typeset by Dorchester Typesetting Group Ltd
Printed and bound in Great Britain by CPI Group (UK) Ltd, Croydon, CR0 4YY

FSC
www.fsc.org
MIX
Paper from
responsible sources
FSC® C171272

1 3 5 7 9 10 8 6 4 2

British Library Cataloguing in Publication data available.

PB ISBN 978-1-911490-75-3
eISBN 978-1-915026-00-2

A MESSAGE FROM CHICKEN HOUSE

The *Vi Spy* trilogy ends with a bang! Vi's mission is: 1) to save the world; 2) to fix her warring parents; and 3) to face up to her beloved gran's serious illness . . . oh, and there's a rocket ride too! Maz Evans is the funniest author and has a deep, heartfelt understanding of how family life works (or doesn't!). She'll make you cry with laughter – and with sympathy too!

BARRY CUNNINGHAM
Publisher
Chicken House

For my dad,
the original Agent Snore
and The Dad Who Loves Me.
From Mazza, with love
xx

Also by
MAZ EVANS:

Who Let the Gods Out?

Simply the Quest

Beyond the Odyssey

Against All Gods

Vi Spy: Licence to Chill

Vi Spy: Never Say Whatever Again

And for younger readers

The Exploding Life of Scarlett Fife

The Wobbly Life of Scarlett Fife

The Stormy Life of Scarlett Fife

THE END . . . ?

As the *Spinneret* glided through space, Umbra looked back on the Earth and finally allowed herself a smile.

She'd done it.

The world – that insignificant pebble behind her – was hers. She glanced over to the box containing the Neurotrol, the tiny microchip that would give her everything. Total control over every adult mind on the planet. Power. Wealth. Victory. Revenge.

Umbra's eyes swept over the vast array of controls on her flight deck. She was perfectly on course for NIDUS, the space station with an antenna that, combined with the Neurotrol, would create the universe's first and only mind-control machine. She was on her way. She was unstoppable.

With no small satisfaction, she found her mind drifting back over the past decade, the ten long years it had taken for everything to come together. It had all gone to plan – well, everything except for Robert and his treachery. She had underestimated the pull that troublesome brat Vi would have on her right-hand man, Sir Charge, and nearly paid dearly for it. But she hadn't. And with NIDUS in her control, she would soon make sure that Robert did. She'd force him to destroy the family he'd chosen over her. No one betrayed Umbra and got away with it.

And then there was Easter. Umbra snorted as she celebrated how easy it had been to fool one of the world's greatest spies. Agent Lynx might have been invulnerable to bullets and bombs – but friendship had proved her weakness. As Honey B, it had been insultingly simple to infiltrate Easter's home and heart. Umbra could have taken her revenge at any moment, of course. But shooting someone while they slept or poisoning them over dinner was for amateurs. Villainy was an art form. And Umbra was a grand master. Umbra had hit Easter where it really hurt – she'd made her enemy look stupid. And that was a wound from which Easter Day would never recover. Robert could take care of Valentine. Easter Day was all Umbra's.

Ensuring that her spacecraft was cruising effortlessly towards her destination, Umbra allowed her eyes to close. World domination was a tiring business – and the next few days would see little chance for rest. She sneezed gently – all this sleepless plotting was giving her a cold. No matter. It was a small price to pay. She allowed her eyes to droop and her mind to float. Soon it would all be over. Soon . . .

A cacophony of alarms snatched her from her doze. She checked the flight deck – was there a malfunction? No, all systems were reporting normally. Umbra fixed on the navigation system. The *Spinneret* was being pulled off course. The shuttle was no longer heading for NIDUS; it was being drawn towards a tiny moon . . .

Umbra frantically tried to override whatever was dragging her, but it was no good. The *Spinneret* was in the grip of something strong, something determined not to let her go. With a curse, she angrily surrendered to its force. She was being pulled to the moon and there was nothing she could do. As her ship entered the moon's atmosphere and sped towards the ground, Umbra looked over at the Neurotrol again. Whatever was attacking her would soon be sorry.

Because Umbra was taking over the world.

And nothing was going to stop her.

CHAPTER 1

'And do you, Easter Day, take this man, George Douglas Sprout, to be your lawfully wedded husband, to have and to hold from the moons of Tatooine to the mountains of Hoth, to love like Leia and to cherish like Chewbacca from this day forth until you are both transported to a galaxy far, far away?'

Vi had to give it to this registrar. At least they had a more interesting script than the previous ones.

Valentine Day had already become something of an expert in weddings at twelve years old, having watched her mother's two failed attempts to marry George Sprout and her nan's one successful one marrying Rod Staff. Perhaps if being a spy didn't work out, she could conduct weddings? It was certainly a safer career choice.

Although judging by her family's weddings, not necessarily . . .

'I do,' Easter smiled, trying to ignore the R2–D2 bleeping enthusiastically at her feet. Vi's mind drifted to Russell's irritating robot with a love of 1980s pop music.

'Come back, Agadoo,' she muttered to herself. 'All is forgiven.'

A gasping sob from her grandmother made Vi look over at Independence Day, who hadn't even had time to dye her hair her customary wedding pink, so quickly had this wedding been pulled together.

'There's nothing like the end of the world to focus your priorities,' her mum had kinda joked as she and George hastily organized their 'intimate' (Vi had quickly learnt this meant 'small') wedding at the only venue they could get with two days' notice – a *Star Wars* tribute hall that had a last-minute cancellation when the groom admitted to the bride that he preferred *Star Trek*. The only guests were immediate family, which according to the bride had two key advantages.

'Well, firstly, it gets round that whole awkward

Do-I-invite-my-best-friend-who-actually-turned-out-to-be-Umbra,' Easter had said. 'And secondly, it saves a fortune on catering.'

Apparently, she was kinda joking again. (Vi had quickly learnt this meant 'it wasn't very funny'.)

Vi shook her head, trying to dismiss any thoughts of Umbra, the world's greatest super-villain, known to them for years as Vi's godmother, Honey B. Umbra would have to wait. Today was about Mum and George – Umbra was tomorrow's problem. Although with Umbra already in space clutching a mind-control device that would give her total domination of the planet, Vi tried not to worry about how many tomorrows they all had.

Another breathless sob from Nan snapped Vi back to the replica deck of the *Millennium Falcon*, as her nearly-stepbrother, Russell Sprout, handed his dad the ring that would finally make Easter George's wife.

'With this ring – a custom that incidentally dates back to the Ancient Egyptians, who saw the circle as a symbol of eternity –' George sniffed, 'I thee wed.'

Vi and Russell smiled at one another as George

placed a ring on Easter's finger. They were finally going to become a family. She watched Rod hand Nan a hankie, which Indy coughed into emotionally. Nan had been looking forward to this day as much as her own wedding. It was sweet to see her so overcome.

'But first,' the registrar said as solemnly as his large Yoda ears would allow, 'I must ask if anyone here present knows of any lawful objection to this marriage. Raise your lightsabers now, or forever hold your peace.'

Vi forced a smile. This had historically been the sticking point with her mum's previous weddings, the first interrupted by the return of Vi's reformed super-villain father, Robert Ford, and the second by George's ex-wife, Genevieve. But today, nothing could go wrong. Everyone here was thrilled for the bride and groom. There wasn't anyone to object.

Though Vi still willed Yoda-ears to get a move on, just in case.

'In which case,' the registrar finally announced with a smile, 'I now pronounce you—'

'I'm so sorry!' Nan suddenly cried out. 'I can't carry on!'

Vi felt her blood freeze in her veins. Surely her nan couldn't object to her own daughter's marriage? They'd all had to sign a pre-wedding declaration promising they wouldn't defect to the dark side, for pity's sake.

'Nan?' Vi exclaimed.

'Indy?' George cried out.

'Lotus Flower?' Rod growled.

'Mum?' Easter yelled.

'Darth Vader?' Russell asked.

Everyone turned to look at Russell Sprout, who simply shrugged.

'Come on,' he muttered. 'It wouldn't be the weirdest thing to have happened at one of these weddings.'

'Mum, what is going on?' said Easter through strained teeth.

'I . . . need . . . to . . . stop . . . this . . . wedding,' Indy gasped.

'FOR CRYING OUT LOUD, MUM!' shouted Easter, throwing her bouquet on the floor. 'All this time you've had to say something and you choose now! I know that things didn't work out with Robert and you said I shouldn't have married him because he's—'

9

'—a complete idiot,' George added enthusiastically.

'Yes, that,' Easter continued. 'And maybe you have reservations about my judgement because of that. But George is a good man. A kind man. He's made me happier than you'll ever know and you need to trust my judgement as a grown woman because I need this man in my life and I just want to MARRY HIM!'

'I know all of that, you daft mare,' Indy gasped, holding on to Rod. 'But I need something too.'

'WHAT?!' everyone cried together.

'An ambulance,' whimpered Nan faintly, leaving Vi watching in horror as her beloved grandmother crumpled to the floor unconscious.

'Why didn't you tell us?' whispered Easter as they gathered around Nan's hospital bed later that afternoon. Vi watched as Nan slipped her fingers through her daughter's. Indy's hand somehow looked much smaller than usual. But maybe Vi's mind was playing tricks on her. She hoped so. Anything was better than what Indy had just told them.

'And just when was I supposed to slip it into the conversation?' scoffed Nan. '*Hi, love, the doctors have given me a few months to live. Fancy a cuppa?*'

'You should have told me,' said Easter unevenly. 'I could have helped you.'

Vi could see her mum was trying very hard not to cry. She felt George's arm slide gently around her shoulders. That made Vi want to cry too.

'A bloomin' wizard couldn't help me now,' Indy grinned. 'My time's up. I've had a good run – more than many I've known in our profession.'

'That's not the point,' said Easter more forcefully, turning to Nan's husband. 'I suppose you knew about this?'

She gave Rod Staff a look that would terrify anyone who wasn't Rod Staff.

'This was your mother's information,' he growled. 'She wanted it to stay on a need-to-know basis.'

'I'm her daughter and I needed to know!' Easter cried, her tears now readily escaping. 'I have a right to know, I deserve to know, I—'

'Well, you know now,' said Nan. 'So let's not waste what time we have left digging over it. It's not quite the end game I had in mind. I'd always hoped to go out more like a supernova than a supermarket candle. But what's done is done. Let's enjoy what's ahead together. And when my time comes, you need to let me go.'

'NO!' Vi found herself screaming before she realized the word was in her head. 'No, no, no! There has to be something – a . . . a . . . medicine or a . . . a . . . an operation or . . . just . . . a . . . something! You can't give up like this! You can't!'

Vi wiped away the tears that were spilling down her cheeks. She didn't care about crying now. She just wanted her nan.

Indy looked at her granddaughter with a kind smile.

'Could you give us a moment, everyone?' she asked.

'I'll stay,' said Easter, wiping away her tears.

'No, you won't,' said Indy firmly. 'You'll do what you're told, madam.'

Vi waited for Easter to fight back, to tell her mum she was staying and that was that. But Easter simply nodded and said nothing. Rod kissed his wife on the head, ushering everyone out of the cubicle. Easter clung to her mother's hand. Then, with a reassuring squeeze and a wink from Indy, she finally let it go.

'I'll be in the relatives' room,' Vi's mum said. 'If you need anything at all . . .'

'You'll be the first to know,' Indy smiled back. 'Now clear off, the lot of you.'

Easter trudged from her mother's bedside, pulling the curtain back around the bed as she left.

'Well, thank goodness for that,' said Nan, heaving herself up on the bed. 'It was getting like Jabba the Hutt's pub in here. Now come here, you.'

She patted the blanket next to her. Vi stuck stubbornly to her spot. This wasn't happening. She wasn't going over there to let her nan talk her into this. She was going to—

A single raised eyebrow from Independence Day informed her she was going to do exactly what her grandmother said.

Vi dragged her feet reluctantly to the bed and sat at the end of it. Nan frowned.

'I realize I haven't had my bed bath yet, but I don't think I smell that bad,' said Nan, sniffing her armpits before gagging. 'Actually . . . *eurgh*.'

A treacherous smile formed on Vi's lips. She hated it. None of this was funny. Whatever her stupid mouth did. There was nothing to smile about. She wasn't sure there ever would be again.

'Get over here, you chump,' Nan commanded, scooting across the bed so Vi could sit next to her. Vi crawled up the sheets and snuggled in next to her nan. Indy did smell – of lavender. Vi hadn't realized how much she loved it until now. How much she needed it. How much she couldn't manage without it . . .

'Now you listen to me, madam,' said Indy sternly. 'You are training to be a spy – and I have a feeling you're going to be our best one yet.'

Vi shrugged as if she didn't care. Largely because she didn't.

'Whatever,' she muttered. 'I might not even bother now. If you're giving up, why shouldn't I?'

'Giving up!' laughed Indy, causing a cascade of coughs that made Vi feel guilty for provoking them. 'Giving up! I made it to old age! I've packed more into my seventy-nine years than most people could squeeze into seven hundred! I've travelled the world – and saved it more than once! I've loved two wonderful men and created two wonderful women! I've lived over twenty-eight thousand days – George told me that – to make these old bones and I wouldn't change a single one of them! So I'm not giving up on anything, missy. I'm celebrating.'

'But how can you celebrate . . . this?' Vi cried. 'You're going to—'

'Die,' said Nan plainly. 'You can say it. You should say it. The more you say it, the less power it has over you. I'm going to die, Vi. That's just part of life, my love. You'll be sad for a while. And then you'll find your joy again. It's the way it's always been. The way it always should be.'

Vi shook her head and snuggled back into her nan. She wasn't going to say it. She wasn't even going to think it. This wasn't happening. She felt Indy's arms pull her closer.

'You are going to be a fantastic spy,' she repeated. 'The very best. But I said it to your mother and I'll say it you: a spy's greatest weapon is their mind. A huge part of the spy adventure is to know who you can save — and to know who needs saving. My mission is nearly accomplished here — and it's been a roaring success. Life is a ticking bomb, darling. At least I know roughly what's left on my clock. Do you understand what I'm saying?'

Vi sat in warm silence with her grandmother as she thought about what Nan had just said. As she turned the words over and over, suddenly it all started to make more sense. She sat up, wiped her eyes and gave her nan a weak smile.

'Yes,' she said. 'I think I do.'

'Atta girl,' said Indy, giving her cheek a big squeeze. 'Now go and get the others so I can say goodbye and get some rest. And tell your mum to bring me something decent from the canteen – the food here is almost as bad as hers . . .'

Vi jumped off the bed and gave her nan a big kiss. She skipped out of the ward and went to find her family in the relatives' room. She was so glad she and Indy had that chat – she was feeling much better now. Nan was right. Her job was to decide who needed saving – so now it was perfectly clear what she had to do:

Vi needed to save Independence Day.

CHAPTER 2

'**Y**EOWCH!'

Vi's hand snapped to her sore scalp for what felt like the thousandth time that evening.

'Really sorry,' said Easter distractedly. She was braiding Vi's hair in Rod's front room – or one of them; Rod's home, Ragnarok, was enormous – while they waited for him to bring Indy home from the hospital. Easter always said that doing Vi's hair helped her to relax. But Vi wasn't finding it very relaxing at all.

'YEEOOWCHCH!' she yelped again as Easter absent-mindedly yanked her hair.

'Really, really sorry,' sighed Easter, who didn't seem to be very relaxed either as she slapped more coconut oil into Vi's hair.

'She's going to be OK, you know,' said Vi

between gritted teeth.

Easter stopped and turned Vi towards her. She looked horribly serious. But it was still more comfortable than the braiding.

'Vi,' she said slowly. 'This is an incredibly difficult time for our family. I know you are hurting terribly – you love your nan so much.'

Vi swallowed hard. Yes. Yes, she did. No need to go on about it.

'But,' Easter continued cautiously, 'we are all going to have to be incredibly strong and incredibly brave and face up to some very hard truths about what is going to happen . . .'

'I know,' said Vi quickly, spinning back around again. 'But you'd better hurry up and finish my braid – they'll be here any minute.'

Vi closed her eyes and waited for her mum's hands to return to her hair. She didn't want to have this conversation. They didn't need to have this conversation. Nan was going to be OK. Vi was going to make sure of it.

She was relieved to feel Easter's nimble fingers start to ring an elastic around the final braid. Or she was until the front door opened.

'YEEEOOOOOWWWWCCCCCHHH!'

she screamed at the top of her lungs as Easter headed for the door, Vi's braid still in her hand.

'Eeeek – really, really, really sorry, baby,' said Easter, rapidly tying the braid off. 'I'll sort out the flyaways later.'

'No rush,' muttered Vi as she got up off the floor. Her mum's bare hands had been bad enough – the thought of Easter attacking her braids with scissors didn't fill her with joy.

Vi made her way towards the grand hall, but as she approached it, she found herself worrying about how Nan would be. Would she be sad? Frail? Ill?

'Oh, get your hands off me, you great lug,' she heard Indy shout from the hallway. 'And you can chuck out this hunk of junk, for starters.'

Vi rounded the corner just in time to see her grandmother kick over the wheelchair in which Rod had wheeled her through the door. Vi smiled. Nan was going to be . . . just Nan.

'Now, will someone please get the kettle on?' she huffed, accepting Easter's hug. 'I couldn't tell the difference between that hospital tea and the contents of my wee bottle.'

'Already on it!' George shouted from the

kitchen. 'Welcome home, Indy!'

'Thanks, Georgie boy,' Nan shouted back. 'Sorry about your wedding, love. I was so excited to officially welcome you into the family.'

'Don't think on it,' George yelled back. 'Did you know that it's considered good luck if a cat sneezes the day of your wedding? Maybe we'll try that next time. And, anyway, families are made from love, not legalities.'

'Well said, that man,' grinned Indy, winking at Vi.

'Are you sure she should be home so soon?' Easter whispered to Rod. 'Surely she needs to be near the doctors?'

'Oi – I'm still here, you know,' Indy snapped. 'And as for those doctors, I've got knickers older than that bunch of babies.'

'She discharged herself,' Rod said – rather proudly, Vi thought. 'That's my Lotus Flower. Knows her own mind. As surely as the world will end tomorrow.'

Vi had noticed that recently, everyone had stopped correcting Rod when he made his grim predictions. With Umbra and the Neurotrol heading towards the powerful antenna on

NIDUS, his theories suddenly didn't seem so out there after all.

'Hey, Miss Indy,' said Russell brightly, giving Indy a big hug and a bigger smile. 'Good to have you back.'

'Good to be back, kiddo,' Indy grinned back. 'Don't suppose you could rustle up some biscuits with your dad's tea, could you? And not those horrible ones with the raisins in. If I want something that tastes like a dead fly, I'll eat Easter's mung bean casserole.'

Vi waited for her mum to tell Nan off. But Easter just smiled and laughed nervously. Unlike Russell, who laughed his head off.

'I'll make sure they're chocolate,' said Russell with a wink. Russell never winked. This was weird. 'Back in a mo.'

'I'll go and help,' said Vi, following him towards the kitchen and grabbing him when no one was looking.

'What's with the Charlie Chuckles routine?' she hissed at her still-not-stepbrother. 'My nan is seriously ill.'

'I know that,' shrugged Russell. He'd been pretty quiet since his unreliable mother,

Genevieve, had ditched him again a few days previously to return to her 'new' family. Which made this weirdly chipper attitude all the stranger.

'So why are you acting like you're watching a pantomime?'

Russell sighed. 'When my grandpa knew he was really poorly, he made me promise that I wouldn't act like he'd died before he had,' he said. 'I'm guessing Indy wants the same thing.'

'Yeah, well, my nan's not going to die,' said Vi defensively. 'So you can stop with the stupid jokes.'

Russell looked away from Vi and hitched up his glasses.

'I'll go and get the biscuits,' he mumbled, and scuttled off towards the kitchen.

'You do that,' Vi grumbled back, although she wasn't entirely sure why.

The sound of screeching tyres and a slamming car door on the driveway outside snapped her out of her funk. As did Easter's unenthusiastic welcome.

'Robert,' she sighed, as a low saxophone melody floated through the door. 'I'm sorry – with everything that's been going on, I'd totally forgotten about your trip, Vi's not even slightly ready.'

'Easter, my dear, don't you worry your pretty little head,' Vi heard her dad drawl as she went to greet him. 'Hello, my darling. How are you holding up?'

'Hi, Dad,' said Vi, suddenly feeling very tearful as her dad pulled her in for a hug. Why was she so emotional right now? It was all going to be OK . . .

'I'm fine,' she said, swallowing down the tears. 'How are you?'

'I'm just marvellous,' Robert grinned back. 'Very excited about our holiday – a bit of sun, sea and shenanigans is exactly what you need.'

'Sure,' said Vi uncertainly. She had been really excited about her first proper holiday abroad with her dad. But now she just really wanted to be near her nan.

'You go and have a good time,' said Indy, as if reading her mind. 'We'll be fine here.'

'Indy!' smiled Robert cheerfully. 'Still alive?'

'Robert!' Indy smiled back. 'Still a complete idiot?'

'That's the girl,' Robert laughed. 'Now let's get you on the road, Miss Valentine.'

'I haven't packed for her yet,' Easter sighed. Vi

looked at her mum properly for the first time in the past few hectic days. Easter looked really tired. Discovering that her best friend was her arch-enemy was tough enough without having to worry about Indy too. All the more reason, Vi figured, for her to make sure Nan got better.

'But we're going to be staying here for a while,' Easter continued, 'so all her things are upstairs. Can you give me a minute?'

'Take several – I'll order us a cab,' Robert grinned, guiding Vi towards Ragnarok's front door. 'I'll just let Siren know – she has a doctor's appointment. I didn't dare ask the details.'

'Hey, kiddo!' called Siren, looking ever glamorous behind the wheel of Robert's car in her red dress, black shades and white headscarf. 'Sorry, I can't hang about, I'm going to get my—'

'Er, sorry, Dave?' Vi asked politely. 'Do you mind? I can't really hear.'

Siren's saxophonist calmly placed his instrument in his lap and pulled his hat over his eyes.

'I SAID,' Siren yelled above the car's motor, 'I'M JUST GOING TO GET MY WARTS LASERED!'

'Tried to warn you,' Robert muttered under his

breath, before turning to the super-villainess. 'You crack on, Siren – I'll phone you later.'

'Have a great trip, you two,' Siren called back as she roared the engine. 'I'll miss you, Robbie – even more than my warts.'

'Um, yes, well, take care of yourself, dear,' Robert spluttered. 'See you when we get back.'

'Laters potaters!' the former villainess winked.

Siren blew a kiss and with the touch of a button, turned Robert's car invisible, a shower of gravel the only marker of its speedy departure down the driveway.

'Er, Dad? Why is Siren driving your car?' Vi asked as they went back into the house.

'Oh, I, uh – I'm just staying with her. Temporarily,' Robert stammered. 'Just . . . temporarily, while, you know, my house is being rebuilt after Umbra blew it up. It's a . . . temporary thing. Temporarily.'

'Temporarily. Got it.' Vi smiled. Stammering was her dad's big tell. Robert was lying.

'So, Rod,' said Robert quickly, adjusting his tie, 'how's ground control?'

'Hmmmm,' Rod growled, as they made their way through to Ragnarok's grand library, where George was laying out tea. 'Amateurs.'

'You're just fed up that they've pinched your favourite toy,' Indy chided. 'They're going to put your *Moonbreaker* to its best possible use. And the sooner you let them get on with their work, the sooner they can get out of here and stop Honey – I mean, Umbra.'

Vi looked towards the bookcase, behind which was hidden the ground control for Rod's beloved spacecraft, *Moonbreaker*. She could hear the hum of SPIDER agents inside, racing around to get their world-saving space mission underway as soon as possible. The moment Rod revealed his self-built rocket to SPIDER, they had immediately 'commandeered it' (Vi had quickly learnt this meant 'took it') to chase after Umbra and stop her from plugging the Neurotrol into NIDUS. The house had been a hive of activity for the past few days as Ragnarok became the nerve centre for the operation to save the world. And Rod was extremely grumpy about it.

'Those kids couldn't stop a dripping tap,' Rod grumbled. 'This is a proper mission. For proper agents. Agents who know what they're doing.'

'I . . . er . . . I don't suppose I could take a peek, could I?' Robert whispered to Rod. 'Always fancied a trip aboard a spaceship. Tried to blow a few up back in the day. But never actually got to go inside one.'

George snorted into his tea.

'Something to add, Georgie?' said Robert with a strained smile.

'It's a space shuttle,' George corrected him. 'Not a spaceship. Extraterrestrials travel in spaceships. Astronauts travel in space shuttles. I know a bit about it. I always wanted to be one.'

'Which one?' Robert quipped with the same nasty grin. 'Astronaut or alien?'

'Nice suit and tie,' George said with a forced smile. 'Are you appearing in court?'

'Oh, I always like to dress sharply, Sprout,' said Robert, straightening his tie. 'You never know what the day might bring. A smart lunch. An important meeting. A wedding – or half of one.'

'Dad!' Vi chided, passing Nan her tea. 'Behave.'

'Idiot,' Nan sighed, blowing the steam off her cuppa.

Robert raised his arms defensively, but said nothing more.

'I always fancied being an astronaut,' said George, clearly trying to rise above. 'The best summer I ever spent was at space camp. I was convinced I could make contact with other life forms — I even built an interstellar communication device out of a matchbox wrapped in tin foil with a cocktail umbrella, so I could speak to extraterrestrials!'

Vi shot her father a warning glare as he smirked into his tea.

'That must have been fun,' Indy smiled.

'It was,' sighed George. 'And the best fortieth birthday present I could have asked for.'

Vi felt her dad draw breath to say something. She stamped on his foot so he wouldn't.

'An astronaut, huh, Sprout? The heck with this — come with me,' growled Rod, wheeling his mobility scooter towards the fake book that opened the secret bookshelf door.

'Oh, Rod, just leave them alone,' Indy huffed. 'Isaac doesn't need you getting underfoot.'

'It's still my rocket,' Rod pouted, pulling the book down. 'And it's still my house.'

'Suit yourself,' sighed Indy, taking a bite of chocolate biscuit.

'Can I come?' asked Russell keenly as the bookshelves started to open.

'I'd love a peek too,' said Robert eagerly.

'Sure. Vi?' Rod said with a smile.

'Yeah – OK,' said Vi with a shrug. She wasn't sure how many chances she'd get to see a real space shuttle in her life. And, she realized with a shudder, she couldn't be entirely sure how much life she had left. With the Neurotrol harnessing the powerful antenna on NIDUS, Umbra would be able to get any adult on the planet to do anything – force countries to start wars, make world leaders launch deadly weapons, turn every grown-up on the planet to violence and chaos . . . She would have complete control of the Earth. The consequences were unthinkable. This SPIDER space mission had to work, for all their sakes.

'I'll catch you up in a minute,' said Nan, coughing slightly. 'You go on.'

Vi looked back at Indy as Rod replaced the book. Her nan was right. Life really was a ticking clock.

And right now, Umbra was holding the timer.

CHAPTER 3

The bookcase parted fully and, as the noise below hit her, Vi had to admit that Ragnarok ground control made an impressive spectacle. From the platform she could see dozens – hundreds, maybe – of SPIDER agents scurrying around the rows of computer screens, shouting complex instructions and typing frantically into keyboards. In the ocean of faces, she could pick out The Wolf – AKA Isaac Payne – the new head of SPIDER and absolved former Umbra suspect.

'This is so cool – let's go and say hi to Isaac,' she said to Russell. 'Russell? Russell?'

Vi looked over to Russell Sprout, but his face – the exact replica of his father's – was frozen, gawping at the extraordinary scene unfolding below.

'Hello! Earth to Planet Geek?' said Vi loudly, waving her hand in Russell's face.

'What? Oh, yeah, Isaac, sure,' he garbled, his hands trembling slightly as they found the familiar bridge of his glasses. 'Let's go.'

They walked – or wheeled, in Rod's case – down the metal ramp and into the hub of the action. If anyone noticed they were there, it didn't stop them from going about their hurried business, meaning it took the family a good few minutes to navigate the crowds and reach The Wolf at the front of the room.

'Agent Redback,' The Wolf greeted them cordially. 'Gentlemen. Kids.'

Vi smiled. The Wolf never used any more words than were entirely necessary.

'How's it going?' Rod asked.

'As fast as we are able – largely thanks to you, Redback,' The Wolf began, eliciting a cordial grunt from Rod. 'Umbra has a head start, but our tracking systems have observed that the *Spinneret* appears to have slowed its progress.'

'Slowed how?' Robert asked.

'We're not sure,' The Wolf replied. 'Our GPS is battling significant radio interference, so we're still trying to clarify the data. At the moment, we're struggling to lock the *Spinneret*'s coordinates. But in any case, *Moonbreaker* is a considerably more sophisticated shuttle than Umbra's *Spinneret*. We're confident that after launch tomorrow, we should make up ground pretty quickly and then we can . . .'

The Wolf's words trailed away as he was approached by a man Vi didn't recognize. He was dressed in a green army uniform and had a flat green hat covering his shaved white head. Vi recalled that this made him high-ranking military. And it looked like this guy wanted everyone to know it.

'You can't be in here!' the soldier snapped at Vi and her family. 'This is a restricted area! And someone get these children out of here! This is ground control, not a playground!'

'General Bark,' The Wolf said firmly. 'This is Agent Redback, inventor of *Moonbreaker* and in whose home we are presently guests.'

'And these children are my family,' growled Rod aggressively. 'So they can play wherever they damn well want, you pompous prune.'

Vi was impressed. Rod still had it.

The general glowered at Vi and Russell but said no more.

'General Bark has been tasked with training an elite squad of military intelligence agents to fast-track them into space,' The Wolf explained.

He gestured towards the group of seven agents, who were variously suspended upside down or being put through their paces on space equipment inside a Perspex gym.

'And a fine job I'm doing too,' the general replied. 'When I'm not being interrupted.'

'Then I suggest you get back to doing it,' The Wolf commanded. 'We are T-minus twelve hours until launch. I'm surprised you have the time to talk to us at all.'

'There are a lot of things that surprise me about this mission,' General Bark smouldered. 'Under my command—'

'—which we are not,' said The Wolf. 'So let's not waste our time on conjecture. This space shuttle leaves tomorrow. Are your team ready?'

'You bet they are,' snapped the general defensively. 'Are you?'

'For anything,' The Wolf glowered. 'I suggest we all go home and get some rest. There won't be much of that over the coming days.'

'Well, we can agree on one thing,' muttered the general.

'We'll reconvene at zero four hundred hours,' said The Wolf, checking his watch.

'Make it zero three hundred,' General Bark growled. 'The early bird gets the Umbra.'

'That's not a thing,' said The Wolf. 'But suit yourself.'

The general snorted derisively, turned on his heel and marched towards his team.

'Well, he's an idiot,' Vi remarked to the general's back.

'We don't use terms like that, Agent Day,' The Wolf reprimanded.

'Yeah,' Rod agreed. 'The technical term is "butthead".'

'I couldn't possibly agree,' The Wolf replied, although Vi swore she saw a slight smile twitching on his lips.

'Quite an impressive operation you have here, Payne,' Robert said, looking around.

'Extraordinary,' George agreed. 'Tell me, will tomorrow be a conventional rocket launch or will you use an air-breathing jet engine?'

'Spare us,' Robert whispered, plenty loud enough for George to hear.

'Apologies if I take an interest,' George snapped.

'You can take anything you want, dearest Georgie,' said Robert smoothly. 'An interest, a photograph, a long walk off a short pier . . .'

Vi nudged her dad. Hard.

'Right, everyone, that's it for today,' The Wolf shouted to the room. 'Go home to your families. Who knows when you'll see them again?'

The exhausted agents didn't wait for further instruction. Machines were powered down, weary bones were hauled out of chairs and in no time at all, the frantic mass of bodies had left and the room was still.

'I'll lock up behind you,' Rod assured The Wolf. 'Good luck with the launch.'

'Thanks,' The Wolf said warmly. 'And thank you again for your invaluable input, Agent Redback. Without you, there would be no mission.'

Rod nodded a gruff acknowledgement. He also wasn't one for many words.

'Well, goodnight, everyone,' sighed The Wolf,

allowing a small yawn to escape him. 'I'll see you tomorrow.'

'Don't count on it,' said Rod, making Vi smile. It was good to have some constants in this very uncertain world.

She watched Isaac Payne make his way slowly out of the room, before turning to join the others in staring at Rod's space shuttle. *Moonbreaker* loomed majestically in front of them, a red-and-silver tower of engineering brilliance, with two enormous metal . . . sausages stuck on the side. She was quite the spectacle.

'She's really something, ain't she?' Rod said proudly. 'Built every inch of her myself.'

'Quite the most extraordinary thing I've ever seen,' said George, awestruck. 'And *I* get to wake up next to Easter Day every morning.'

'*Dad,*' Russell chided, as George shot Robert a smug look.

'So,' whispered Rod, peering around to check they were alone, 'who fancies a closer look?'

Vi laughed and waited for everyone else to join her. But no one did.

'I'm serious,' said Rod, checking over his shoulder again. 'It's my rocket. Who wants to take a peek inside?'

'Are – are we allowed?' George gasped, his eyes the size of satellite dishes.

'Don't be such a square, Georgie,' said Robert, striding off towards *Moonbreaker's* launch pad. 'Unless you're a scaredy cat.'

'I am no such thing,' huffed George, puffing out his chest. '*Some* of us just play by the rules.'

'And *some* of us just enjoy the game,' Robert smirked back. 'After you, Agent Redback.'

Rod trundled his mobility scooter across ground control and over to the thermally insulated launch pad that would send *Moonbreaker* into space. Robert skipped after him. Vi watched George and Russell's inner excited geeks wrestle with their inner law-abiding citizens for all of five seconds before they followed behind.

They all made their way to the launch pad and stood at the foot of the massive rocket.

'Wow,' said Russell, and it was the only thing to say. This close, the rocket was vast and even more impressive.

'However did you build it?' George asked, taking an admiring stroll around the base.

'Time,' sighed Rod. 'Like all young folk, I

thought I had more of it than I did. Always dreamt of taking this baby into space as its commander. The design is revolutionary – I built it to self-launch. Made sense, given I figured I would be the only human being alive on the planet to use it.'

'You did?' George asked. 'But how is that even possible? How would it work? How do you operate it?'

Rod grinned and leant towards George.

'Do you want to find out?'

Vi honestly thought that George Sprout would self-launch there and then. She'd never seen him so giddy. Except possibly when he won that back-stage tour of the Science Museum from the school Christmas tombola.

'Come on,' Rod cajoled, wheeling towards the platform that would take them up to the rocket's nose cone. 'It's OK, I know this baby inside out and back to front.'

'I'm game,' said Robert, leaping on to the platform.

'Dad?' Russell asked. 'You don't have to if you don't—'

But whatever Russell was suggesting was lost entirely to the tornado created by his father racing to join the others on the platform. Vi and Russell shared a smile and followed their fathers.

'You surprise me,' said Robert, jostling for space on the small platform. 'I didn't have you down as having a backbone, Georgie.'

'And yet I always had you down as a bonehead, Robert,' sighed George.

'You ready?' Rod said with a schoolboy grin, his finger hovering over the button.

Everyone nodded.

'In which case—'

'WHAT IN THE BLUE BLAZES DO YOU THINK YOU'RE DOING?'

Vi couldn't imagine that many things scared Rod Staff. But the sound of his new wife screaming across the launch pad seemed to do just the trick.

'Lotus Flower!' he cried. 'I was just . . .'

'You were just being a silly old fool is what you were just being,' said Indy, hobbling over with her stick and giving him a swift poke in the ankle as she boarded the platform.

'Sorry, baby,' Rod pouted.

'So you should be,' said Indy. 'How dare you go without me? Are we going up to this rocket or not?'

Vi gasped. Rod grinned.

'Nan!' Vi exclaimed. 'You should be in bed, resting.'

'Oh, hush, I'm fine,' she said, scowling at Vi's shocked face. 'Bored off me brains, though. And, besides, I've heard Rod go on about this tin can that much, thought I might as well see what all the fuss is about. Up we go.'

Rod took Indy's hand and kissed it, before prodding the button hard with his finger.

'Onwards and upwards,' he said as the platform shuddered to life. Vi watched as the ground dropped beneath them and the rocket towered above. Time with her family was certainly anything but dull. She smiled at Russell and he smiled back. This was so—

'VALENTINE DAY!'

This was so over.

'Mum!' Vi called down to Easter a few metres below. 'It's OK! We're only looking!'

'At a classified space shuttle that is scheduled to save the world tomorrow!' said Easter. 'And as for you, Mother – you get down here now! All of you!'

'Sorry, kid,' Rod called below. 'Can't override

the lift mechanism. We'll have to go up to come back down.'

'Oh, for goodness' sake,' Easter huffed. She turned around and stepped away. Vi was surprised to see her back down so easily. But she forgot that this was Easter Day.

With a few bounding strides, Easter raced across the launch pad and jumped against the rocket, propelling herself the few metres she needed to grab on to the bottom of the rising platform.

'Mum!' Vi cried again, watching her mother dangle from the ascending lift.

'Vi – chill,' Easter replied, rolling her eyes as she heaved herself easily up to the platform, where George quickly helped her aboard. 'If I can do it on a helicopter above the Grand Canyon, I can certainly do it here.'

Vi didn't ask. She wasn't sure she wanted to know.

'Now, put this thing back on the ground!' ordered Easter, as the platform continued its jerky ascent.

'I told you, I can't,' said Rod plainly. 'This is usually a one-way trip, remember? I'll have to disconnect it at the top, so that it knows to go back down. Won't take a minute.'

'Relax, darling,' said Robert, stretching his arms out along the rail. 'What could possibly go wrong?'

'Where you're concerned, anything,' said Easter, putting her arms around George. 'And I am NOT your darling.'

Vi and Russell rolled their eyes in sync.

'Parents,' muttered Russell.

The platform rose up the height of *Moonbreaker* until, after what seemed like a very long journey, it reached the hatch that the astronauts would use tomorrow to enter the capsule. Rod opened a control panel on the rocket's side.

'From memory, the switch to disconnect the platform is . . . this one!' he said triumphantly, as the hatch opened instead. 'Or not.'

'So this is what the inside of a real space shuttle looks like!' gasped George reverently, peering into the open hatch. 'It's a bit more impressive than the simulator at space camp. I never thought I'd see the day . . . '

'Well, you're not seeing it today,' said Easter firmly. 'Rod, disconnect this platform and take us back down. Now.'

'Sure thing, boss,' said Rod with a small salute. 'If it's not that button, it must be . . .'

Rod flicked another switch. Vi clung to the handrail as the platform lurched away from *Moonbreaker*. The good news was that this time he'd found the one that operated the platform. The bad news was that George was now leaning so far into the hatch, he completely lost his balance — and fell headlong into the capsule.

'GEORGE!' Easter cried, clinging over the edge. 'George! Are you OK?'

'I'M INSIDE A SPACE SHUTTLE!' George shouted back jubilantly. 'YOU BET I'M OK! ALTHOUGH I MIGHT BE A BIT STUCK!'

'Of course you are,' Easter sighed. 'Hold on — I'm coming in.'

Rather more elegantly than her fiancé, Easter climbed over the edge of the hatch and entered the capsule. Vi and Russell rushed to the opening to see what had become of both parents.

The inside of the capsule was like a car, if it were standing on its exhaust pipe. The seats were positioned so the astronauts were on their backs, staring up to the sky. Made sense, she figured. If you were going to be fired into space in an over-sized bean can, it probably made sense to see where you were going. George's unscheduled arrival into the capsule meant that he was wedged inelegantly between two of the seats, where Easter was struggling to free him.

'Could use a little help here,' she strained, George's bottom pressed up against her face.

'At your service,' said Robert with waggling eyebrows, moving between the two children to clamber into the hatch. As Easter and Robert worked to liberate George from the seats, the image of her biological parents trying to free her nearly-stepfather was not something Vi was likely to forget. Even if the language they used while they were doing it was something that she probably should.

'If you'd just listen to me,' Robert strained.

'If you'd just use your biceps as much as your jaws,' Easter strained back.

'There!' cried Robert as a red-faced George finally popped out from his trap, allowing him to pull himself on to one of the upwards seats. 'You're denser than you look, Georgie.'

'You're not,' said a breathless George, resting in

the seat behind him.

'Me next!' said Indy, tottering over to the hatch.

'Mother! Don't you dare!' said Easter from the back of the shuttle, from where she'd had to push George out. 'We're all getting straight out.'

'When am I going to sit in a space shuttle again?' Indy asked. 'You're not going to deny your old mum a dying wish, are you?'

Vi winced. She didn't care for her nan's turn of phrase.

Though she did have to admire her style.

'Oh, go on, then,' said Easter. 'But quickly.'

'Tee hee – come on, kids, lend a hand,' said Nan, with a wicked twinkle. It was the liveliest she'd looked all day. Vi and Russell helped her up into the hatch, while Robert helped her inside.

'And I thought the sun was the oldest thing in outer space,' he quipped as she settled herself into her seat.

'And I know you're the most idiotic thing in any space,' said Indy, waving up at the kids.

'Well, go on,' said Rod, gesturing to Vi and Russell to get inside. 'You might as well – everyone else is in there.'

'Are you . . . are you sure?' Russell asked, one leg already over the hatch.

'Never surer,' winked Rod, his crinkly face gracing them with a rare smile.

Vi and Russell grinned happily as Russell, then Vi climbed inside.

'Incoming!' yelled Rod just behind them as he heaved himself into the capsule with his arms alone. Vi was impressed – he was stronger than he looked. With Robert and George's help, Rod made his way into the commander's chair, which Vi observed was also built like a mobility scooter.

'OK, you've had your fun,' said Easter, calling from the back of the capsule. 'It's time to— Wait, what's happening, what are you—'

Vi looked around nervously as the small space started to darken.

'Relax,' said Rod as the capsule door shut behind him. 'I'm just giving you all a piece of what it's like to be real astronauts.'

'Well, I'm going to give you a piece of my mind if you don't open that door,' said Easter. Vi noticed a slight panic coming into her voice. 'I don't do well in small spaces, I feel like . . . I can't . . . breathe . . .'

'Don't worry,' said Rod, flicking another switch. 'I designed this capsule to be like one giant space suit – you'll have all the oxygen you need.'

'What does this button do?' Robert asked, jabbing a button next to him.

'Don't do that!' George snapped. 'This is a highly sophisticated piece of machinery, you don't know what you're doing.'

'Like this?' said Robert, pushing another button.

'Robert, stop it!' said Easter, sounding properly panicked now. 'This isn't a toy!'

'What – even this one?' said Robert, flicking a switch.

'Dad!'

Vi turned round and shot her dad a warning stare. He was being epically childish.

'I'm telling you, Robert, don't mess with what you don't—' George began.

'Oh, lighten up, Georgie,' said Robert, stretching his arms with a yawn. 'I'm only going to press—'

'Stop it!' shouted George, slapping Robert's hand away from the controls on the capsule ceiling. But as Robert's hand jerked to avoid him, his left thumb hit a big green button above them.

Suddenly, the whole capsule sprang to life, lights flying on with an overwhelming chorus of beeps and bloops, screens flashing strings of numbers and a juddering rumble shaking the very ground beneath them.

'What's that?' Vi panicked, as Rod started frantically pushing buttons on his dashboard.

'Oh, nothing,' said Rod breezily as the noise from below got louder.

'*ENGINE THRUSTERS ACTIVATED*,' a computerized voice informed them. '*LAUNCH SEQUENCE INITIATED*.'

'So it *was* an air-breathing jet engine launch,' George mused under his breath.

'Not now, Dad,' Russell whispered, a definite tremble in his voice.

'What?' Easter panted. 'What engine thrusters? What launch sequence? What . . . whatever George just said? Rod, shut this thing down!'

'Don't panic, everything's under control,' Rod said smoothly, his fingers whizzing around the controls on the console. 'It's just a test sequence, nothing is going to—'

'*PREPARING FOR LAUNCH*,' the voice contradicted. '*LAUNCHING IN TEN . . . NINE . . .*'

'Rod?' said Vi, looking nervously around the capsule. 'Rod? What's happening?'

'*. . . SEVEN . . . SIX . . .*' the computer continued.

'Nothing I can't handle,' said Rod. 'But maybe put your safety belts on – just in case.'

'SAFETY BELTS!' Easter squealed, while fumbling to strap herself in. 'Why would we need—'

'*. . . FOUR . . . THREE . . .*'

Vi looked over at Russell, who had gone deathly pale as he strapped on his belt. She felt his hand reach for hers. Was this . . . was this really happening?'

'*. . . TWO . . . ONE . . . BLAST OFF!*'

The huge roar of the engine confirmed what the computer had already told her.

This was really happening.

'ROD! ROD!' Easter screamed. 'We're moving off the ground! What's it doing? Where are we going?'

Rod stopped his jabbing, turned around and grimly faced his family.

'Sorry, folks,' he said calmly. 'It looks like we're going into space.'

CHAPTER 4

'**W**HAT DID YOU DO?' Easter screamed at Robert as *Moonbreaker* blasted away from Ragnarok and accelerated upwards through the night sky.

'I didn't do anything!' Vi's dad exclaimed, yelling over the ear-splitting noise inside the capsule. 'It was Sprout – if he hadn't slapped me . . .'

'If you hadn't been behaving like a naughty toddler, I wouldn't have had to!' George yelled back. 'This is all your fault!'

'Brace yourselves,' said Rod from the commander's seat. 'The boosters are about to peel off.'

'What does that—' Vi began to ask, before a giant bang answered her question. She clung to her seat as the flight deck was bathed in a flash of light and the two metal sausages broke away from *Moonbreaker*'s main body. Vi felt as if half her class were standing on her chest, the immense weight pushing her back into her seat.

'What was that?' Easter whimpered at a huge clank. 'And that? And why is it doing that? And what was—'

'Stay cool, Agent Lynx,' Rod commanded. 'Everything is going according to plan.'

'Plan?' Robert cried. 'Plan?! We're blasting into space, man! Whose plan was that?'

'Just sit back and enjoy the ride,' said Rod. 'We'll be entering orbit in three . . . two . . . one . . .'

The capsule stopped juddering and Vi felt the pressure lift from her chest. It felt a bit like when an aeroplane had taken off and everything goes quiet before you take your seat belts off. Although, as Vi's body floated up against her straps, she realized that they were the only thing stopping her from floating around the shuttle. She was weightless.

They were in space.

'You OK?' she asked Russell.

'I think so,' Russell replied, looking around the

flight deck. 'You?'

'Uh-huh,' said Vi uncertainly.

Rod hit another button to open a small compartment on the console, from which he removed a small silver star. Vi could just make out the word *Commander* engraved in its centre. He attached it proudly to his leather cardigan.

'So here we are,' said Rod – Vi sensed this was more to himself than everyone else. He hit another button and the panels around the capsule slowly withdrew to reveal huge windows behind them. Vi looked outside to see Planet Earth spreading out beneath them like a giant marble against the sparkling landscape of space. This might be the most terrifying moment of her life. But it was also the most spectacular.

'Whoa!' said Russell and George at the same time.

'Er, excuse me,' said Easter quietly. 'Lovely as this view is, would someone mind telling me HOW THE UTTER HECK WE GET OUT OF THIS THING AND BACK DOWN TO EARTH?'

'Why don't we ask Georgie? He's the expert,' said Robert childishly.

'Dad!' Vi scolded.

'Why don't you push another button?' George snapped back. 'That worked well last time.'

'*Dad*,' Russell whispered.

'I'm telling you, I didn't push the button – you did!' Robert raged.

'I did no such thing!' George insisted. 'This is all your fault!'

'No, it's not!' Robert retorted.

'Yes, it is!'

'No, it's not!'

'Is!'

'Isn't!'

'Is!'

'Isn't!'

'Is, is, is!'

'Isn't, isn't, isn't!'

'ENOUGH!' came a roar from the front. Vi nearly leapt out of her seat. But it wasn't Rod who was shouting at them. It was Indy.

'Now, listen here!' she yelled, turning around to face her family. 'We have a bit of a situation on our hands, so I'd say we have more important things to figure out than who pushed a bloomin' button! We have work to do. Important work. So, you pair, BUTTON IT!'

Vi watched Robert and George squirm uncomfortably as they muttered discontentedly to themselves. It reminded her of when she and Russell got in trouble for squabbling in the back of the car.

Revenge was sweet.

'Right,' Indy continued with a sigh. 'Rod, can you turn this hunk of junk around and get us back on the ground?'

'Not that simple, Lotus Flower,' Rod growled, his eyes firmly fixed on the way ahead. '*Moonbreaker* isn't a holiday jet – she's used all her fuel for take-off.'

'So, you're telling us that we don't have enough fuel to land?' said Easter, trying to stay calm. 'We – my whole family – are stuck in this . . . metal monster, until we run out of fuel and just end up floating around space for ever?'

'Well, for one thing, you don't need to worry about floating around space for ever,' Rod said.

'At least that's something,' Easter said, holding on to the wall and breathing a heavy sigh of relief.

'No,' said Rod. 'Once the fuel runs out, we'll have no oxygen. We'll all die long before we start floating around space.'

Easter said nothing, but let out a small whimper.

'Well, that's just marvellous,' said Robert, sitting back with his head in his hands.

'How long will our fuel last?' Indy asked. 'How long have we got?'

Rod smiled and kissed her hand.

'At least until tomorrow,' he said with a wink.

'Wait!' said George, suddenly shooting his hand up. Once a teacher, always a teacher. 'When I was at space camp, we learnt about space stations. The space programme was abandoned some years ago, but I recall there are some still-active ones — couldn't we go to one and refuel?'

'Atta boy, Sprout,' said Rod admiringly. 'I'm making you my co-pilot.'

'You're doing WHAT?' Robert cried as George puffed up like a peacock. 'I object . . . no, I refuse . . . no, I insist . . . no, I—'

'You'll pipe down and do as you're told,' said Rod in a tone that even Robert wasn't going to argue with. 'Sprout has experience and we need to refuel. When SPIDER developed NIDUS and its space programme, it launched a small space station, *Spiderling*. It was intended as a drop-off point for supplies, new crew and – crucially – refuelling. It's been abandoned for decades, but as it was never used, everything we need should still be there. I'm setting the course for it now.'

'Well, that's all right, then,' sulked Robert. 'We'll go to this big petrol station in the sky, fill up the tank and get home in time for tea. SPIDER can have their rocket back and they can get on their way after Umbra.'

'Uh, not going to happen, Rob,' said Rod, as George snorted.

'Why not?' asked Vi. It sounded like an excellent plan to her.

'Space shuttles are a single-use item,' Russell explained quietly. 'Once we re-enter the Earth's atmosphere, most of *Moonbreaker* will burn up. There won't be anything left for SPIDER to launch.'

The family fell silent as the heavy reality settled upon them. Vi's mind started to turn it all over. If they went straight back to Earth, no one could defeat Umbra. Once the Neurotrol was connected to NIDUS's giant antenna, Umbra would be unstoppable. Vi's family would be safely on Earth. But they would have put the rest of the population in unspeakable danger. Vi couldn't bear the thought. They were a family of spies – with the odd reformed super-villain. They were supposed to save the world, not endanger it.

A different plan started to take shape in Vi's mind. A new plan. The right plan.

'Or . . .' she began quietly.

'Or what?' Nan said with a familiar twinkle in her eye.

'I'm just saying – and hear me out, Mum –' she added as Easter took an almighty breath – 'that inside this shuttle, we have three retired agents, two trainee ones, a criminal mastermind—'

'A *former* criminal mastermind, thank you, young lady,' Robert corrected.

'Sorry – a former criminal mastermind,' Vi continued. 'And a man who knows more about space than ET. Perhaps . . . perhaps we should be going after Umbra ourselves?'

'No,' said Easter firmly. 'Absolutely not. Our mission priority is to get safely back to Earth. We're not trained for this.'

'Who is?' Rod growled. 'It's not exactly a stand-ard assignment. We've got as good a shot as those meatheads back at Ragnarok.'

'No, no, no,' Easter said again, her hands under-scoring her point. 'This is far, far too dangerous – you might be trainee agents, but you two are still children—'

'—who have survived several encounters with Umbra already,' Russell said quietly.

'Dad used to work for Honey – Umbra – whoever. He knows her better than anyone,' Vi said more confidently. 'No one knows *Moonbreaker* better than Rod.'

'You got that right,' Rod grunted.

'Russell is smarter than most adult techies, Nan can break any code, and there isn't anything George doesn't remember about . . . well, anything,' said Vi.

'Thank you, sweetie,' said George gratefully. 'Although did you know that Suresh Kumar Sharma holds the current world record for recalling pi to over seventy thousand decimal places?'

Easter looked long and hard at her daughter.

'And you and I?' she asked. 'What's our role in this ridiculous idea?'

Vi grinned at her mum and shrugged.

'Honey pretended to be your best friend for

ten years,' Vi said. 'She lied to you, betrayed you, tried to kill you.'

'And so?' Easter pressed, her jaw twitching.

'And so,' Vi concluded. 'We kick Umbra's butt.'

Easter snorted a laugh in spite of herself. She looked at the starry sky outside.

'Agent Lynx,' Rod growled from the control panel. 'You are the only active agent in the field. The world is facing a terrible threat. Could you really return to Earth knowing you missed the opportunity to save it?'

Easter sighed and stared out of the shuttle window.

'How far is it to this . . . *Spiderling*?' she asked.

'About three hours,' Rod replied.

'Good,' said Easter. 'Because if I'm going to survive space, save the world and kick Umbra's butt, I really need to have a wee.'

'General Bark,' The Wolf said abruptly as he walked into Ragnarok in the early hours of Monday morning.

'Agent Wolf,' the general replied sharply. 'You're late.'

The Wolf looked at the clock, which showed two seconds past three a.m. Upon reflection, Isaac Payne had to agree with Rod's preliminary character assessment of the military man before him.

He really was a massive butthead.

'As you know,' General Bark began as they walked down the hallway towards the library, 'I applied for command of this mission.'

'And as *you* know,' The Wolf replied, 'you weren't granted it. This is a SPIDER mission. It will remain under SPIDER's control.'

'I will be keeping a very close eye on proceedings,' the general glowered as they approached the library. 'Those are my people going up there. I need to know they are safe. I'm not afraid to go up the chain of command. As head of SPIDER, I know you answer to Agent Bird, who in turn reports to Agent Cat, then Agent Dog, before Agent Cow reports to the top – Old Lady.'

The Wolf stopped short.

'What happened to Agent Horse?'

General Bark looked horrified.

'She's dead,' he said. 'Of course.'

The Wolf nodded, before resuming their brisk stride towards the bookcase. They could hear a hubbub inside as General Bark moved the book that opened the secret room.

'You can watch as closely as you like,' said The Wolf proudly as the bookcase opened. 'At SPIDER, we pride ourselves on our professionalism, our duty of care and our attention to every single detail—'

His speech was interrupted by a panting junior agent practically falling into his arms from the other side of the bookcase. She was a young woman who Isaac remembered as being particularly impressive during training, even if her personal presentation was a bit messy – today, loose strands of her long black hair were fanning out wildly from her brown face.

'Agent Money?' The Wolf asked. 'Whatever is the matter?'

'Sir – I was just coming to find you,' she gasped. 'We have a . . . situation.'

'I'm sure it's nothing we can't handle,' said The Wolf, shooting the general a confident stare. 'What's the problem?'

'I . . . I . . . don't really know how to tell you,'

Agent Money stammered.

'Spit it out!' the general barked. 'We don't have all day!'

'Well, sir — sirs,' Agent Money blathered. 'It's *Moonbreaker* — it's . . . it's . . .'

'It's WHAT?' The Wolf shouted, immediately regretting losing his cool in front of the general.

Agent Money looked mournfully at her two superiors.

'Sir,' she finally gulped. 'It's gone.'

CHAPTER 5

'**N**ow, the thing about docking,' George announced enthusiastically from the pilot's seat, 'is that in order to rendezvous effectively, we need to arrive in the same orbit and within visual contact of *Spiderling*. Both vessels are travelling at an orbital velocity of 28,000 kilometres per hour – and given that we are in a vacuum, it is critical that we achieve a secure connection.'

George Sprout nodded enthusiastically at his family. Russell smiled back. Everyone else merely gawped.

'Can anyone here translate Geek?' Robert asked.

'Basically, docking is a pain in the butt,' Rod growled. 'So don't mess it up.'

'That's what I said,' muttered a hurt George to

Easter, who patted his shoulder reassuringly.

'So where is *Spiderling*?' Vi asked as she stared out into the boundless darkness around them. She was actually quite excited to see a real space station, which she imagined would look something like a giant space castle floating around Earth.

'Coming up on your two o'clock,' Rod said, flicking some switches on the control panel.

Vi looked out again. The only thing she could see on the horizon was something that looked like the top of a television aerial, consisting of a long tube with massive paddles coming off each end. It reminded her a bit of something she might throw together in design technology. On a really bad day.

'Wow!' said Russell, squealing a bit. 'She's awesome.'

Vi looked again. There was nothing apart from the TV aerial. Surely that couldn't be . . .

'*Spiderling*,' said Rod proudly. 'I was part of the team that designed her. Never thought I'd get to meet her in person. She was cutting edge back in the nineties. Our robotic manipulator system was the envy of the space travel community.'

'Does she have a toilet?' said Easter, who had been very quiet but extremely wriggly for the past hour.

'Nearly there, love,' said Indy reassuringly, just the way Easter had said it to Vi on countless car journeys. Vi had never really considered that Nan was Easter's mum, in exactly the same way that Easter was hers. If Vi was this sad about the possibility of losing her nan, she could only imagine how Easter must feel about losing her mum.

Which was all the more reason why Vi wasn't going to let it happen.

'*Spiderling* is unmanned, so we have no one to help us dock – we're on our own, Sprout,' said Rod to George. 'Do you think you can handle it?'

'Can we take a vote?' muttered Robert, earning him his umpteenth warning look from Vi.

'Sure,' said George. 'At space camp we simulated the docking process many times. I'm sure the old grey cells will still remember some of it.'

'You ain't at space camp now, Sprout!' Rod barked. 'This is a highly critical mission! There is no margin for error! If we don't dock this baby properly, we could cause untold damage to *Moonbreaker*, compromising her safety and the lives of everyone on board! We could all die, Sprout! Do you understand! DIE!'

George froze at the control panel. Rod turned around and took in the pale and shaking faces of his family.

'But we probably won't,' he added, jabbing at some more buttons. 'At least, not today.'

'I believe in you, Dad,' said Russell with a quiet force. 'You can do this.'

'I agree,' said Vi, giving her nearly-stepfather a smile that she hoped was more reassuring than it felt. 'You've got this, George.'

Vi watched as George Sprout visibly puffed up. She heard her dad use a word that would have got her into a lot of trouble if she'd said it.

'We're coming in hot,' Rod announced into his headset. 'You ready, Sprout?'

'Born ready,' said George confidently. 'What do you need?'

'You're in control of the Orbital Docking System,' said Rod, hitting yet another switch, bringing a picture of something that looked like a metal flower with three petals up on the screen. 'Once we're attached, I can activate the base ring to lock in.'

'Roger that,' said George.

'It is absolutely crucial that we align perfectly with *Spiderling*,' said Rod, a little worry creeping into his voice for the first time. 'If we don't, we risk dissipating the docking load with an asymmetrical latch.'

'What does that mean?' Vi asked.

'We'd face major damage to our craft and *Spiderling*,' Rod explained. 'Which probably means that we'd all—'

'Yes, yes, we know,' Indy chided. 'We're most likely to die from boredom if you two don't get on with it!'

'Sorry, Lotus Flower,' said Rod, blowing her a gentle kiss. 'Sprout, do you have control of the Orbital Docking System?'

'I do,' said George, a small film of sweat forming on his brow.

'Do you have visuals on *Spiderling*'s docking interface?'

Vi peered out of the window. On the surface of the *Spiderling* was a . . . sticky-out bit that she could see was designed to fit with the . . . flower thingy on *Moonbreaker*.

'Can you see?' Russell said, leaning over her.

'The docking interface on *Spiderling* locks with the Orbital Docking System on *Moonbreaker*, forming a seal that will allow us to board.'

'I know,' snapped Vi. 'I just thought the exact same thing.'

'Affirmative,' said George, wiping his forehead as *Spiderling* loomed larger ahead. Vi tried taking a deep breath to calm her racing heart. It didn't work.

'Initiating thrusters,' Rod announced, and Vi immediately felt *Moonbreaker* start to slow – although even in her amateur estimation, not quite enough.

'It's . . . it's coming up very quickly,' said Easter nervously, echoing Vi's thoughts.

'You're off target,' said Robert as *Moonbreaker* inched closer to the space station.

'Once you allow for the energy transfer, we'll align,' George said, the sweat pouring freely down his face.

'I'm telling you, man!' Robert said more forcefully. 'You're not going to make it!'

'Yes, I am!' said George, *Spiderling* now approaching them at terrifying speed.

'Robert – let him concentrate!' Easter scolded

at a volume that would make concentration very tricky.

'My only child is aboard this vessel!' Robert shouted.

'So's mine!' George shouted back.

'Will you be QUIET!' Indy shouted at Robert. But Vi could see her dad was not for turning. She looked over at Russell, whose faith in his father looked less certain than it had a moment ago.

'Er, Dad?' he said quietly. 'Do you think you should . . .'

'You see!' said Robert triumphantly, unlocking his belt and floating towards the console. 'Even his own son doesn't trust him! Move aside, Sprout! I'm taking control!'

'Robert! Sit down!' Easter shouted.

'DAD!' Vi added, trying to grab her father as he floated over the seats.

'Sir Charge!' Rod roared, using Robert's villainous pseudonym. 'Stand down! Your insub-ordination is endangering us all!'

'Respectfully, Commander Redback, I can't agree,' said Robert, trying to wrestle George for his seat. 'I have no confidence in the command of this vessel and I'm taking control.'

'SIT DOWN!' Rod roared.

'I WILL NOT!' Robert roared back as the now enormous *Spiderling* filled the screen in front of them. The pointy bit was sticking right out at them, like the barrel of a gun.

'*DOCKING IMPACT IMMINENT,*' *Moonbreaker's* system informed them. '*COLLISION DETECTED. BRACE, BRACE, BRACE.*'

'Just let me do it!' Robert shouted, grabbing George's arm.

'I'm already doing it!' George shouted back, wriggling free of Robert's grasp. 'You're going to make me lose my—'

'*IMPACT PREDICTED IN THREE . . . TWO . . . ONE . . .*'

'Hold tight, everyone!' Indy echoed, pushing her stick against the shuttle wall for stability.

Vi braced herself and felt her mother's hand on her shoulder. She tried to close her eyes, but couldn't resist seeing what was in store as *Moonbreaker* crashed into *Spiderling* with almighty force. Everyone was thrown forward – the unharnessed Robert into George – and there was a terrifying pause as they all waited to see if the vessel around them was going to split apart at the force of the impact, sucking them all out into the deathly blackness beyond . . .

But it didn't.

For a moment, no one said anything, the gratitude of still being alive giving them a moment to release their collective breath.

Though, as was often the case in Vi's family, the silence didn't last long.

'You are a complete IDIOT!' George roared, slapping the large lump of Robert floating on his lap.

'Told you so,' muttered Nan, patting down her hair and smoothing her dress.

'You could have killed us all!' George continued, as Robert clambered out of George's lap and floated back to his own seat.

'Well, if I hadn't intervened, you *definitely* would have killed us all!' Robert shouted back.

'Did we get the lock?' Russell called over the noise of the two grown men. 'Rod? Are the two vessels latched?'

Rod was busy jabbing away at the control panel, the screen running multiple checks.

'It's not a great latch,' he growled, holding up his glasses to better peer at the screen. 'But we're on. No thanks to Tweedledum and Tweedle-dummer here.'

'IT WAS ALL HIS FAULT!' both men said at once, pointing at each other.

'I don't care whose fault it was!' Rod yelled back, making everyone jump. 'If I ever see behaviour like that again, I'll eject you both into space myself. Sprout Senior, you are relieved of your post. Sprout Junior, you're now my pilot!'

'Who, me?' said Russell incredulously. 'You want me to ... fly *Moonbreaker*?'

'I do,' said Rod.

'But ... why?' Russell asked.

'Because you are one of the best damn technicians I've ever met,' Rod said dispassionately. 'Because you're smart and you know when to take orders. Because I know you can do it. And, frankly, because everyone else would be as much use as a hedgehog in a balloon factory. No offence.'

'None taken,' beamed Indy, winking at Russell.

'Well – OK, then,' said Russell. 'If you're sure ... Commander.'

'I am,' said Rod decisively, turning to Robert and George. 'And as for you two – we got lucky this time. But nothing else interferes with this mission, do you understand me? Nothing!'

Vi was reminded how scary Rod could be when he was angry. It certainly seemed to work on George and Robert, who immediately shut their mouths and stared grumpily at the floor. There was an embarrassed silence.

'I really need that wee!' came the urgent whisper from Easter as Rod released the airlock at the back of the capsule.

'And you shall have it,' said Rod, undoing his seat belt and turning around to address them all. 'Our objective is to locate the supplies we need for the mission and head for NIDUS. Umbra has a head start, but we can still catch up. Now, remember, we are in a microgravity environment. Everything floats. Boys – I don't have my scooter up here, so can you lend a man a hand?'

George and Robert pouted grumpily, still smarting from their ticking-off.

'You heard the man!' Indy commanded. 'Do something useful for a change!'

'Wait. When you say "everything"?' Vi asked as she released her safety belt. 'Do you mean—'

Her question was quickly answered as her

straps fell away and she gently left her seat.

'Whoa! This is . . .' she spluttered as her whole body was lifted into the air.

'Whoooopeeee!' Indy squealed as she too floated out of her seat.

She watched Robert and George each take half of Rod and guide him awkwardly to the tiny airlock, into which they all just about squeezed, Easter still jiggling away mid-air. Rod shut the doors behind them.

'This is EPIC!' Russell declared as his glasses started to float around.

'There are rails on the ceiling,' said Rod with a grin as he floated to the other side of the airlock to release the doors into *Spiderling*. 'Helps you to get around. And . . . here we are.'

The doors to the other side of the airlock opened and Vi stared straight into what looked like the inside of a computer. The walls and ceiling were covered with old wires and ancient screens and keypads and clocks and buttons and . . . she didn't even know what half of it was. She had images of the space stations she'd seen on TV and the movies – all slick and high-tech. No wonder those people had made those ones up.

This place was a mess.

'OK,' said Rod. 'Let's split up and try to find the kitchen module. *Spiderling* was designed to hold a rotating crew of eight for twenty-five years, so there should be plenty of supplies – only the crew that originally stocked it have been here since it was built. Lotus Flower, you come with me. Kids, you go that way. Easter – the bathroom is right here, you'll need to remember that in a micro-gravity environment, liquids will—'

'MOVE ASIDE!' cried Easter, propelling herself along the roof rails and locking herself into the tiny compartment to their right.

'And you pair of knuckleheads go wherever you want,' Rod said to Robert and George. 'Just stay out of each other's way.'

'Suits me,' said George, floating off straight ahead. 'Why don't you loosen your tie, Robert. Might let some more blood flow to your brain.'

'Don't get lost, Georgie!' Robert shouted after him as he took a tunnel to his left. 'Actually, on reflection . . . do!'

'We'll rendezvous back here in thirty minutes and get on our way,' Rod said. 'Touch only what you need. And be careful.'

'LOOK AT ME!' Indy cried, turning a somersault mid-air.

'Nan – be careful!' Vi scolded.

'Oh, quit your worrying,' said Indy, turning the right way with a big grin. 'This is FUN! What a day.'

Vi looked at her nan with concern as Russell chuckled at Indy's somersaults.

'I don't know why you're smiling,' said Vi, as they grabbed their way to the next module. 'She's seriously unwell.'

'And right now, she doesn't feel it,' said Russell, trying to catch the glasses that were still floating around him. 'So I think that's something to smile about.'

Vi huffed, but decided to turn her attention to finding the kitchen module. If they were going to catch Umbra, they needed their strength. And now she thought about it, she was really hungry.

'What do you think it looks like?' she asked Russell as they worked their way from one module to the next. 'The kitchen?'

'It'll look like everywhere else,' Russell answered. 'But it'll have food in it.'

Vi stopped to give him a withering look. He just laughed.

'What's so funny?' she said.

'Your hair,' said Russell, trying to push his glasses back on his face again. 'It's sticking up.'

Vi put her hand to her head and could feel her braids pointing due north. She didn't find it nearly as funny as Russell.

'Just look for the food,' she grumbled, her stomach joining her. 'I'm starving.'

They carried on floating through the space station with the help of the guide rails, passing endless computers, wires, panels and plugs on all sides of the narrow corridors. Everything was brand new, yet really old. It was a bit spooky. Vi hurried along – she wanted to get out of here.

'What was this place for?' she asked Russell as they floated through to yet another module.

'It's basically one giant science lab,' Russell answered enthusiastically. 'Space offers a unique environment for conducting experiments. They make all kinds of advances – science, technology, medicine . . .'

'Medicine?' said Vi, her ears pricking. 'You mean they might have medicines up here they don't have on Earth?'

'Would have done,' said Russell gently. 'Remember, no one has been here for thirty years.'

Vi tried not to let another ray of hope extinguish. She was going to help her nan. No matter what.

'I think I've found it!' Russell said breathlessly, pointing to a display of plastic bags on the wall.

Vi floated over to join him. She'd never really thought about space food before – she figured that they just ate out of the fridge like everyone else. But what greeted her was an array of flat, metallic packets, labelled by food type – meat, cereal, drinks, snacks and so on. She felt her stomach rumble. They didn't look very appetizing.

'What's this?' she asked as she pulled a metal packet out of one of the plastic bags. She heard Russell gasp behind her.

'Er, Vi?' he said.

'Spaghetti bolognese?' said Vi, reading the label.

'Vi . . . Vi,' Russell said, tugging her arm.

'Macaroni cheese,' said Vi doubtfully, reading another.

'*Valentine!*' Russell repeated, tugging at her arm harder.

'Calm down. These all look disgusting,' said Vi, ignoring the pull at her sleeve. 'And I've eaten Mum's cooking for twelve years.'

'Oh, they're not so bad once you rehydrate them,' said a new, male voice behind her, nearly making her jump out of her skin. 'But, honestly, the lasagne's much, much nicer.'

CHAPTER 6

'AAAAAAAAAARRRRRRRRRRGG-
GGGGGHHHHHHHH!'

Vi remembered watching a film once that said,
'In space, no one can hear you scream.' She really
hoped that wasn't true.

'AAAAAAAAAARRRRRRRRRRRGGGG-
GGGHHHHHHHH!' she screamed again at the
top of her lungs as she turned to see a middle-
aged white man, with possibly the worst haircut
she'd ever seen, sitting at a table behind them. So
in case it hadn't worked the first two times, she
screamed again.

'AAAAAAAAAARRRRRRRRRRGGGG-
GGGHHHHHHHH!'

'Oh, I'm so terribly sorry,' said the man, floating out from under the table to come over to

Russell and Vi. 'I didn't mean to startle you. It's been a while since I've had any guests. I must have forgotten my manners.'

'Who . . . who are you?' Russell managed to splutter out as Vi prepared to scream again.

'My name is Theodore Logan,' said the man politely. 'But please – call me Ted. All my friends do. If I remember rightly.'

'VI! VALENTINE!' came a breathless shout as Robert tumbled into the module. 'Are you OK?'

'I – I'm not sure,' said Vi more calmly, as she looked at Ted's gently smiling face. He didn't exactly look like a murdering maniac. But then he wouldn't really have had the chance up here.

'Who are you?' Robert demanded.

'I'm Ted,' said the astronaut, holding out a friendly hand. 'How lovely to have you here.'

'You OK, kid?' came Rod's familiar growl as he and Indy bundled into the now rather crowded module. 'And who are you?'

'Still Ted,' laughed Ted amiably. 'Gosh, if I'd known we were going to have a party, I'd have made a freeze-dried cake! Welcome aboard *Spiderling*, everyone. Delighted to have you.'

'Kids!' came George's worried cry from behind

everyone. 'Is everything all right? Who are—'

'He's called Ted,' said Vi to save time. 'And we think we're fine.'

'You must all be exhausted after your journey,' said Ted, gesturing to everyone to sit – or at least strap themselves down – at the table. 'Can I get you a cuppa?'

'Oooh – don't mind if I do, Ted,' said Indy gladly, taking her place at the table. 'I'm spitting feathers.'

'I bet,' said Ted, floating over to the plastic bags and pulling out a series of foil pouches. He injected one with hot water and handed it over to Indy.

'I'm afraid it's not exactly high tea at the Savoy,' said Ted, 'but it's better than nothing.'

'Much obliged to you,' said Nan with a smile as she raised her pouch to him before Ted went about getting refreshments for everyone else. Vi watched her nan giggle as she examined her space tea.

'You see,' whispered Russell. 'She's having fun.'

Vi had a general policy of not agreeing with Russell about anything. But even she had to admit that her nan did seem to be having a great time. She gratefully accepted a pouch of water and a kind of . . . dehydrated ice cream from Ted. The shock of seeing him – and his wild grey hair – had possibly made her even hungrier. She squeezed her water pouch and a blob of liquid floated out in front of her in a giant bubble.

'Oh!' she gasped, wondering how she was going to drink it.

'All liquids do that here,' Ted explained as he passed around some dehydrated biscuits. 'It makes drinking so much more fun! Look . . .'

'Cool,' she whispered as she followed Ted's example and swallowed the bubble whole.

'Is this what you call bubble tea?' Nan quipped through a mouthful of biscuit. 'Geddit? Bubble tea? Anyone? Ah – suit yourselves, I'm wasted on you all.'

'So, Ted, I have to ask—' George began, swallowing a bubble of coffee.

'What in the blazes are you doing here, man?' Rod roared. 'This station was supposed to be empty!'

'Well, it's a bit of a funny story, actually,' chuckled Ted. 'I was part of the crew who came up here to establish the station in 1997 and ready it for passing space travellers on their way to NIDUS.

I've never been much of a people person, so there was I just quietly getting on with my work one day, when I only saw the space shuttle I arrived on, blasting back to Earth! You could have knocked me down with a feather!'

'So . . . they left you here?' Russell asked, a bubble of juice escaping him. 'On purpose?'

'Oh, I don't think there was any malice in it,' Ted mused, swallowing another bubble. 'I'm just one of those people who fades into the background. You know, someone people barely notice is there, someone who—'

'So let's get the supplies and get out of here,' interrupted Robert. 'We need to— WHOA!'

Robert ducked just in time as a large computer flew over his head.

'Oh, yes,' Ted chuckled. 'I should warn you about that. You need to watch out for low-flying objects around here — professional hazard, I'm afraid!'

'Haven't you gone completely out of your mind being up here all this time, all by yourself?' Vi asked. 'No one to talk to, nothing to do . . .'

'Like I say, I never was much of a one for company,' smiled Ted. 'Not that it isn't lovely to have you all here – what a treat! And there's plenty to do on a space station, believe me! Tests to run, repairs to make, novels to read. I mean, I've written most of the novels myself, but at least that means they're all ones I like! I suppose I'm a little out of touch. I hope things are a little more sensible down there – they were talking all kinds of silly when I left! Everyone was going on about this "World Wide Web" and how we'd all be doing everything on screens in the next ten years! Can you imagine? Can't think that caught on.'

Ted ducked as another giant computer floated past his head.

'But . . . but . . . aren't you furious with your crewmates for leaving you?' Vi pressed. She couldn't honestly believe that someone could spend almost thirty years inside this flying circuit board and be happy about it.

'Not at all!' said Ted. 'I've lived a very happy life here. Many people dream of living in space. I've actually been able to do it. And I've learnt all sorts of skills I'd never have learnt at home – just look at this hair! Did it myself! Can you believe it?'

Vi looked at the wonky and lopsided grey hair.

Yes. Yes, she really could believe it.

'You see?' whispered Nan with a wink. 'Not everyone needs saving.'

Vi scowled. She didn't want to spend another minute here – let alone the next thirty years.

'So how can I help you all?' Ted asked amiably.

'We're in pursuit of a notorious super-villain who is trying to control Earth with a mind-control device called the Neurotrol,' Robert explained. 'We can stop her – but we need supplies for the mission.'

'Oh dear – what a palaver!' said Ted, drinking another bubble of tea. 'Well, of course, help your-selves. There's so much more here than I need, you'd be welcome to whatever you want—'

A sudden jolt made them all lurch, bubbles of tea, coffee and water floating all over the module.

'What the heck was that?' Nan asked, trying to grab her last drop of tea from a foot above her head.

'Sounded like it came from the docking station,' Ted said, typing something into an ancient computer. 'Did you have any trouble parking?'

'No. Thanks to me,' said Robert smugly.

'Oh, good, then I'm sure we have nothing to

worry about,' said Ted, picking up another biscuit.

'Where's Mum?' said Vi, realizing that they hadn't seen her for a while.

'When you gotta go, you gotta go,' said Indy with a wink. 'Maybe she just needs a moment.'

'Um, hi,' came Easter's familiar voice from the module around the corner. 'I could do with some . . . advice.'

'Surely,' said Ted, floating towards Easter. Vi followed on to make sure her mum was OK. 'What can I do for you?'

But as she and Ted rounded the corner, Vi couldn't help giggling. Looking much more comfortable, but extremely embarrassed, was Easter. And floating around next to her was a very big, very yellow bubble.

'Um, excuse me,' a blushing Easter whispered. 'Could you please explain to me how to flush the loo?'

An hour later, greatly refreshed for some food, drink and correct use of the toilet facilities (it wasn't an experience Vi wanted to repeat any time soon, but it involved using a special space hoover somewhere a hoover should never go), the family was getting ready for Ted to refuel *Moon-breaker* so they could head off for NIDUS.

'It's been a real pleasure, Ted,' said Rod. 'We'll be sure to let ground control know you're here. Perhaps they can send someone to get you?'

'Oh, no rush,' said Ted pleasantly. 'I'm still working my way through the DVDs of series one of *Friends*. Wouldn't Ross and Rachel make a lovely couple? Can't see it, though . . .'

'Well, we'll be on our way,' said Robert, walking back into the airlock. 'Thanks so much for—'

Another almighty jolt suddenly hit *Spiderling*, this time setting off a whole orchestra of alarms.

'DAD! QUICK!' said Vi, grabbing her father by his arm just as the airlock snapped shut. 'What's going on?'

'OK – no one panic,' said Ted, his fingers flying across another computer keyboard. 'It seems we've had a teeny, tiny problem with your shuttle. It didn't dock correctly—'

'TOLD YOU SO!' said Robert and George simultaneously to one another.

'And so, we've sustained a little bit of a bump to

one of the oxygen cylinders,' Ted explained calmly. 'I'm sure it's just a scratch, though – I've seen it all in my time here, let me tell you. I'm sure it's nothing to worry about.'

As the alarms continued to blare around them, a voice echoed through the space station.

'*WARNING, OXYGEN SUPPLY COM-PROMISED. WARNING, OXYGEN SUPPLY COMPROMISED.*'

'What?' Vi and Russell said together. That definitely sounded like something to worry about.

'This is all your fault!' said Robert and George together.

'Stop all talking at once!' said Easter and Rod together.

Nan looked around at her family before floating over to Ted.

'Now I'm no expert here, Ted,' she said quietly. 'But I'd say that oxygen supplies might be a bit of a problem up here.'

'Only if they run out,' said Ted brightly. 'We should have plenty of time to fix the problem before that happens.'

'*WARNING: OXYGEN SUPPLY CRITICAL. WARNING: OXYGEN SUPPLY CRITICAL.*'

'It never rains, it pours,' trilled Ted, still tapping into the computer. 'So, there's bad news and good. It looks like there is indeed some significant damage to an oxygen cylinder. I'm going to have to go on a little spacewalk to patch it up.'

'Good grief,' said Robert, running his fingers through his hair. 'What's the good news?'

'Oh – that *was* the good news,' said Ted brightly. 'The bad news is that we're going to have to get a bit of a wriggle on if we're going to do it in time.'

'How much time?' Rod asked. 'I'm guessing tomorrow ...'

'Well, that would be nice!' giggled Ted. 'No, I'm afraid we're going to have to be a bit nippier than that.'

'How nippy?' George asked nervously, floating over to take Easter and the children in his arms.

'Ooooh, we just need to make sure we get out into space, fix the damage and get back inside before total oxygen failure.'

'And how long is that?' asked Vi, not really wanting to hear the answer.

Ted looked back at his screen before smiling benevolently back at the group.

'If we're lucky?' he mused. 'Slightly under an hour.'

'*Moonbreaker!*' The Wolf shouted for the thousandth time that day. 'Come in, *Moonbreaker!* This is ground control requesting an immediate situation report! *MOONBREAKER!*'

Isaac Payne threw down the headset in frustration. How had this happened? Agent Lynx and her family were nowhere to be found. Had he really misjudged another colleague? Were they all actually in it together with Umbra? Had he been fooled again?

But his gut answered the question before his brain had to. He knew Easter. She was a good person and a great agent. Wherever she was, she would always be working for SPIDER.

'Agent Wolf,' came the breathless voice of Agent Money. 'We've managed to retrieve the security footage from Agent Redback's computer – it was super-encrypted, it's taken a whole team most of the day to break it.'

The Wolf withheld a rueful smile. He'd

recognize Agent Labyrinth's work anywhere.

'What did you find?' he asked.

'I'm afraid it's not good news, sir,' Agent Money spluttered. 'Our worst suspicions are confirmed. Agent Lynx and her family are aboard *Moonbreaker*. They must be in league with Umbra.'

'Agent Money!' The Wolf snapped. 'There is presently no proof of anything and I thank you not to throw damaging and unfounded allegations around about one of our top agents.'

'Sorry, sir,' Money muttered. 'I was just—'

'You are just supposed to do your job!' The Wolf barked. 'You're not here to cast aspersions on Agent Lynx's motivations.'

'But I am,' came the equally unwelcome contribution from General Bark. 'This whole agency is a joke! First, you harbour Umbra under your own noses for a decade, before letting them kill your predecessor. Then you let their second-in-command, Sir Charge, steal our only shuttle to join them! The whole family must be in on it.'

'There is absolutely no evidence at this stage that Agent Lynx, nor any of her family, are in league with Umbra,' The Wolf reiterated.

'But what about Robert Ford?' the general

replied. 'I know he used to be Umbra's right-hand man. Looks like old habits die hard.'

'The extended Day family has been critical to the unmasking of Honey B and are just as determined to bring her to justice as I am,' The Wolf said defiantly. 'I'm certain of that.'

General Bark took a menacing step forward.

'Are you, Wolf?' he questioned in a low growl. 'Are you certain? Because it seems to me that SPIDER is rotten to the core. And you could be the worm that's festering in the middle.'

The Wolf took a menacing step of his own.

'Keep talking, General,' he threatened, 'and it will be my pleasure to show you just how rotten I can be.'

The two men froze in a tense stand-off.

'Um, shall I leave you two to it?' Agent Money whispered. 'OK, I'll just ... be ... over ...'

She scuttled away, leaving the two men eyeballing one another intensely. The general was the first to break.

'It's become quite clear to me and many others that your leadership has been completely compromised by this turn of events,' he declared. 'It would obviously be in everybody's best interests if you stood aside and let me assume command until a full investigation can take place.'

'We don't have time for a full investigation,' The Wolf smouldered. 'As far as we're aware, Umbra is already on her way to NIDUS.'

'Thanks to your agency's incompetence,' the general added. 'You don't even know for sure where she is.'

'But to my knowledge, at this stage, I have an agent in pursuit,' The Wolf continued. 'The mission is going ahead as planned. And until I have reason to think any differently, I believe that Agent Lynx is working for us and she is our best hope of stopping Umbra before it's too late. As you said, General, those are my people up there. She is my agent, this is a SPIDER mission – and you are a colossal butthead.'

The general recoiled, but didn't rise to the bait. The Wolf wished he had – a show of temper from the general would give him grounds to have him removed from the building and out of harm's way. But right now, harm was feeling very close indeed.

'Don't get too comfortable,' growled the general. 'Because if I have anything to do with it, you'll be out of here before the morning.'

'Go and play with your toy soldiers,' The Wolf retorted, putting the headset on again and turning his back on the general. 'Some of us have work to do.'

He could feel the general seething behind him, before hearing angry footsteps storm through ground control. The Wolf had bought himself a bit of time. But would it be enough?

'*Moonbreaker*?' he repeated. 'Come in, *Moonbreaker*?'

He waited for a response. Still nothing.

'Come on, Easter,' he said, more to himself than the headset. 'Where are you? We're running out of time.'

CHAPTER 7

'**W**e're running out of time!' Robert yelled as Ted slowly pulled on his space suit.

'Oh, don't worry too much about that,' said Ted, gesturing to the large computer screen showing the depleting oxygen supplies at forty-eight minutes and thirty-four seconds. 'That thing's such a Grumpy Gus at the best of times!'

'There,' said George, helping Ted into the final part of the massive space suit that would both protect him from the burning and freezing temperatures outside while providing him with oxygen and water. 'Are you ready?'

'Oh, yes,' said Ted happily, pulling on his gloves. 'I pop out there pretty regularly, in fact. There's always something needs a bit of TLC – back when my colleague Asha was here, we used to float out there just for the fun of it.'

'Hate to rush you, Ted,' said Easter, looking again at the clock. 'But, you know, tick tock . . .'

'Yes, of course,' beamed Ted. 'I will chatter on – it's just lovely to have someone chatter back. So it looks like your bumpy landing damaged the emergency oxygen canisters outside the airlock. With so many of us here now, we're using more of the air on board, so the system's running a bit low. I can patch it up, no problem.'

'You're sure?' Robert asked uncertainly.

'As sure as my Game Boy will never go out of style!' Ted insisted. 'That thing's a technological marvel. Now, where did I put my helmet, it'll be floating around here somewhere – you can't miss it, it's such a massive great big old—'

'LOOK OUT!' shouted Russell a millisecond too late, as the helmet crashed straight into Ted's head. It was a big blow.

'Ted? Ted? Are you OK?' Vi asked the smiling astronaut.

'Oh, absolutely,' he slurred. 'Anyone fancy a trip to the cinema? They're showing that new cartoon, *The Lion King*, at four-thirty.'

And with that, Ted floated backwards, totally unconscious.

'Oooops,' said Rod, grabbing the astronaut to stop him drifting around the cabin.

'Ted! Ted!' Vi called, slapping him around the face. She felt her guts knot. Without Ted, they couldn't fix *Spiderling*. They hadn't yet refuelled *Moonbreaker*, so they couldn't escape. And he was the only one who knew where the space ice cream was. They needed him.

'TED!' Russell yelled in his ear. But it was no good. Ted was out cold.

Everyone looked around at each other, waiting for someone to come up with a plan. Rod was first to suggest one.

'So which one of you chumps is going out there?' he said.

'What?' Easter cried. 'Spacewalks are tough on even the most highly trained astronauts! They are incredibly dangerous – there is no way we can do it. Someone could get killed!'

Rod looked up at the clock. Forty-two minutes and twenty-four seconds.

'You got a better idea?' he growled.

'I'll go,' Robert announced, grabbing Ted and

starting to pull off his suit. 'Rod, you can talk me through it.'

'I'm going with you,' came a firm voice behind them. 'We spent time in space suits at space camp – they are complex pieces of machinery. Ted had plenty of experience – we don't. Spacewalks always happen in pairs. For everyone's safety.'

They all turned to face a determined George Sprout.

'Dad?' Russell asked. 'You can't go out there. Especially not with—'

'Robert? With you, George?' said Indy incredulously. 'No disrespect, but the only space you two have in common is the massive one between your ears.'

'Thanks, Georgie,' said Robert, removing Ted from his suit. 'But I work alone.'

'Sprout's right,' said Rod in the tone that wasn't to be messed with. 'You go together. You watch each other's backs. And not so you can stick a screwdriver in them. We need another suit.'

'Ted mentioned his colleague, Asha,' Russell recalled. 'So there must be another suit here somewhere.'

The family split off hurriedly around the space

station. With so few possessions aboard, it wasn't long before Indy called out.

'Found it!' she said, as they made their way back towards the airlock. 'But it's not all good news.'

Vi's stomach lurched. They were standing in a space station that was about to lose its oxygen supply. They didn't really need any more bad news.

'What's wrong?' Easter asked.

Nan held up the petite space suit.

'I don't think Asha and George wear the same dress size,' she said.

'Brilliant,' Easter groaned. 'None of us can fit in that.'

Vi felt her spy instincts click into gear.

'I can,' she said plainly.

'Absolutely no—' Robert began.

'Not a chance in—' Easter agreed.

'What is it you are trying to protect me from?' cried Vi, pointing at the clock. 'If we don't fix this oxygen supply, we're all going to die. At least this way, we have a fighting chance.'

Even her parents didn't have a comeback. It was a hard argument to beat.

'She can do it,' said Russell, smiling shyly at his

nearly-stepsister. 'I know she can.'

'Let the girl go,' said Indy confidently. 'She's proved herself before. She can do it again. I have every faith in her.'

Vi smiled at her nan. Indy always had her back. And Vi was going to make sure she always did.

'I'll be your techie,' said Russell. 'I can help you. I did a voluntary extra credit on technology in zero-gravity environments.'

'Of course you did,' grinned Vi. 'Come on – help me into the suit.'

'Well, I'm going with you,' said Robert. 'There's no way you're going out there without a parent.'

'No,' said Rod firmly. 'Sprout's our man for this mission. You stand down, Ford.'

'I will not!' Robert insisted. 'She's my daughter and—'

'She's our daughter,' Easter interrupted. 'And George loves her like his own. He'll take care of her – and he's the better man for the job.'

'For any job,' Nan muttered, winking at George.

'Enough chit-chat, we don't have time!' Rod commanded as Robert and George eyeballed each other. 'Sprout, Vi – suits on. Young Russell, I'll back you up on comms. The rest of you?'

'Yes,' said Robert, puffing up, ready for his assignment.

'Get out of the way and be quiet. You're no use to us here,' Rod ordered, grabbing a floating computer and gesturing for Russell to do the same.

'Come on, Ted,' said Indy, pulling the unconscious astronaut by his feet. 'We'll go and get the kettle on. They'll need a stiff cuppa when they get back.'

Nan winked at Vi and blew her a kiss as she moved out of the capsule. She never was one for big goodbyes.

Easter helped George into the assorted pieces of the massive suit and Robert helped Vi into hers. It was incredibly heavy and uncomfortable. And so, so hot.

'These suits are extraordinary,' said George admiringly. 'They have everything – oxygen supplies, water cooling systems, they protect you from space dust – they even have a jetpack in the back so you can fly through space! Did you know that without one, you'd only survive fifteen seconds out there?'

Vi felt a bit of sick come up her throat. She really didn't need that geeky fact. Nor to puke in her suit.

'All I need to know is that it's going to keep my girl safe,' Robert grumbled. 'And that you are too.'

'Affirmative,' said George, smiling at Vi. 'We've got this.'

'Yeah, we do,' said Vi with a confidence she didn't entirely feel.

'Don't you be a hero,' said Easter, holding George's face in her hands. 'You come back to me.'

'Like I could ever leave,' said George, accepting Easter's passionate kiss.

'And I thought running out of oxygen was the worst thing up here,' muttered Robert, stifling a retch.

'Now the key objective is to fix up that cylinder and get back in here as quickly as possible,' Rod said. 'Mind out for jagged edges on the ship – even the slightest tear to your suit would mean a race against time before the oxygen around your body evaporated and you blacked out. All the water in your body would vaporize, your lungs would collapse and your circulation would shut down. It's an ugly way to die.'

Vi gagged again. Easter gave Rod a shove.

'Oh,' said Rod flatly. 'I'm sure that won't happen to you – probably. You both stay tethered to the station at all times,' he continued, showing them the metal ropes in the airlock that would attach them to *Spiderling*. 'That way, if anything happens, we can reel you in. George, you need to secure the patch in your suit to the oxygen cylinder outside.'

'Roger that,' said George, trying to salute, but finding his arms wouldn't reach his head in his massive suit.

'Vi, your job is to protect George,' said Rod. 'Make sure he is safe and get the two of you back here stat, you copy?'

'Affirmative,' said Vi, because it sounded like the most official thing to say.

'Then let's get on with it,' said Rod. 'Good luck.'

Vi smiled as Rod floated back towards his computer with no show of visible emotion. Clearly he wasn't one for goodbyes either.

'Vi . . .' Easter began, taking one of her massively gloved hands.

'Valentine . . .' Robert continued, taking the other.

'I've got her,' said George, putting his arm around her shoulder as much as the suits would allow. 'I swear it.'

'You better had,' said Robert darkly.

'I do,' said George, standing up to Robert's steely glare.

'Airlock is prepped and ready,' said Russell. 'You need to get your helmets on.'

Vi took a deep breath as Easter lifted and secured the massive helmet on top of the suit. She tried to quell the panic rising up within her – inside the suit she suddenly felt trapped and distant from her family. This was a terrible idea. What was she doing?

'*WARNING: OXYGEN SUPPLIES WILL END IN THIRTY MINUTES,*' the computer informed them all.

Vi swallowed down her fear. That's what she was doing. She was saving her family.

'Agent Day. Sprout. Can you hear me?' came Rod's voice through the helmet.

'Copy,' said George.

'Copy,' Vi copied.

'Then let's get this show on the road,' said Rod. 'Russell, have you accessed the shuttle schematics?'

'I have,' Russell confirmed as Vi and George walked into the airlock. 'Once you're in the air-lock, there will be thirty seconds' depressurization when you leave, thirty seconds' repressurization when you come back. It is essential you remain in the airlock during this time, otherwise you will get decompression sickness.'

Vi shrugged. That didn't sound so bad.

'It can kill you,' Rod added.

That sounded worse.

Vi looked at George, who gave her a reassuring smile as the doors started to close.

'WE LOVE YOU BOTH!' Easter shouted after them.

'FOR CLARITY, I JUST LOVE VI!' Robert shouted quickly as the airlock doors shut behind them and the thirty-second timer started to tick down. Vi could feel her heart drumming. She was about to go into space. She wasn't even allowed to go into a swimming pool unaccompanied. And yet she was about to go into space.

'Did you know,' George began, securing her

tether as the airlock timer passed twenty seconds, 'that because of the design of these suits being sealed at the neck, if you farted inside one, you wouldn't be able to smell it?'

'I did not,' smiled Vi, more grateful than ever to have her nearly-stepdad at her side. And for a piece of information that could prove more useful that she really wanted to admit.

'It's going to be OK,' George said reassuringly, tethering himself. 'I promise.'

Vi smiled again. But she wasn't nearly as convinced by this one.

They both looked over as the counter ticked down its final numbers.

Three . . . two . . . one.

The massive doors ahead of them opened up to reveal the most extraordinary sight Vi had ever seen.

Planet Earth.

The view from *Moonbreaker* had been incredible – but seeing it here, unobstructed, like this . . . She could see where the sun had risen and where it had already set. She could see light jumping off mountains and the dark void at the heart of oceans. Down there, it was the people who took centre stage. Up here, it was the planet itself. It was beautiful. It was majestic. It was . . . really big.

She looked over at George, who was frozen to the spot, awestruck.

'This is . . . I just . . . I've dreamt of this moment since I was a child,' George whispered. 'It's . . . everything.'

'Sprout!' came Rod's sharp tones inside their helmets. 'This isn't a sightseeing trip. Focus on the mission!'

'Aye–aye, Commander,' said George. 'You OK, Vi?'

Vi nodded, even though as she looked over the edge of the airlock, she realized that she really, really wasn't.

They took some slow, heavy steps across the airlock, Vi tugging on her tether to make sure she was safely attached to the space station. They stood on the edge of the platform, with literally nothing ahead of them.

'You ready?' George asked, rubbing her back with his massive hand.

'Ready,' said Vi and with a deep breath, took one small step.

'So, Dad, now you need to reconnect the feeder tubes,' Russell commanded inside the helmet.

'Vi, can you pass me the pistol-grip tool?' George asked, starting to sound worried for the first time. The repair was more complex and taking longer than they had hoped, and Vi was thinking of the timer ticking down inside. That, and the fact it was quite boring floating here handing George the tools.

'Darn it!' said George in as close to a swear as he ever got. 'It's not working. What's Plan B?'

'Can you reach the bipod assembly on the furthest cylinder?' Russell asked, anxiety creeping into his voice too. 'I think I've found a workaround.'

George reached around the cylinder – but his tether was just too short.

'I . . . can't get to it,' he said, straining as far as his heavy suit would allow. 'If I could just untether myself.'

'That's a negative, Sprout, in the hardest possible terms,' said Rod. 'If you float off into space, you're no use to any of us. Hold your position. We'll find another way.'

Vi could feel the panic starting to rise up again. What if there wasn't another way? If George couldn't fix the problem, their whole family would die aboard *Spiderling*, while they waited for the oxygen in their own suits to run out. Vi looked at the big black expanse ahead of her. It seemed a very lonely place to spend her last moments.

'What news?' said George urgently to Rod and Russell after a painfully long few seconds. 'What can I do?'

'Sit tight,' Rod said. 'Your boy's working on it.'

'We don't have time!' said George with uncharacteristic temper. 'This is ridiculous – I have a jetpack on my suit, I can just float over to where I need to be.'

'I repeat, that is a firm negative, Sprout,' Rod commanded. 'You stay put.'

'*WARNING: OXYGEN SUPPLIES CRITICAL. FIFTEEN MINUTES UNTIL TOTAL SYSTEM FAILURE,*' Vi heard the computer announce in the background. They hovered there helplessly, awaiting instruction.

'This is ridiculous,' George suddenly declared. 'I'm not going to hang around here while everyone I love – and Robert – runs out of oxygen. Rod, I'm deploying my jetpack.'

'Stand down, Sprout!' Rod barked back. 'You are not authorized to proceed!'

'Whatever,' George muttered back, going to untether his suit.

'George!' Vi cried, a huge wave of nausea rising up her throat as she watched her nearly-stepfather disconnect himself from the only thing attaching him to safety.

'Vi, it's fine,' said George, unfastening a controller from the front of his suit. It looked like a joystick on an old-fashioned computer game – she had the same one on hers. 'This will navigate me over to the far cylinder. I can do the repairs and be back in a minute. You wait for me here.'

'What – what are you doing?!' Vi shouted as George floated away from the tether and activated his jetpack.

'I'm being a hero,' George declared. If she hadn't been so scared, Vi would have had to admit that was a pretty cool line – she'd never thought of George Sprout as a hero before. She barely recognized her nearly-stepfather.

'Which, incidentally, originates from the Greek word '*heros*' and means protector or defender,' George added.

And . . . there he was.

'Be careful,' she said to him as he gently blasted towards the far cylinder, using the controller to steer himself through the endless darkness. Her heart was ready to go on a spacewalk of its own, beating as hard as it was in her chest. She watched her geeky stepdad, after a couple of wobbly moments, expertly guide himself the few metres he needed to position himself for the repair.

'That must have been one heck of a space camp,' she muttered to herself.

'I'm here,' he said, as he made contact with the cylinder. 'What do I do?'

'OK, Dad, first you need to disable the electron gas analysers, then you need to bypass the signal and command unit and move to auxiliary power,' Russell instructed.

'Nice one, Junior,' Vi heard Rod grunt approvingly. Compliments from Rod were rare. Russell must be doing a good job. That helped her feel slightly better. But only slightly.

As George worked, Vi found herself holding her breath. This was always the moment in movies where things went wrong, when in a moment of high drama and a race against time, the stakes pile against the hero, the odds seem insurmountable, disaster is—

'Done it,' George announced calmly, closing the cylinder up again.

'*OXYGEN SUPPLIES RESTORED,*' Vi heard the *Spiderling* computer announce. '*CHARGING TO FULL CAPACITY.*'

Wow.

That was quick.

'You did it!' she yelled at George. 'You ARE a hero!'

'Well . . . not really,' George blustered. But even through his space suit, Vi could tell he was blushing. 'Thanks, Russ.'

'No problem, Dad,' Russell replied. Vi could hear the smile in his voice. 'Just get back here safely.'

'Great job, Agent Day, Sprouts, Junior and Senior!' Rod barked down the line. 'Return to base immediately.'

'You bet!' said George, blasting his way towards

Vi, who was eagerly waiting to retether him to *Spiderling*.

'Darling, you were amazing!' Easter gushed. 'Just incredible – I'm so ...'

A worrying bleeping started ringing in Vi's ear.

'What's that?' she snapped. Bleeping was never good.

'Dad,' said Russell, his voice trembling. 'Your suit is reporting a pressure drop. You need to get back on your tether – now.'

'It's ... OK ... son ... nearly ... there,' panted George.

'What's going on?' Vi demanded.

'It's Dad's suit,' said Russell. 'He's losing pressure. If he's not careful, he will lose consciousness. Get him back on the tether so we can pull you both back in. Quickly!'

'Roger that,' said Vi, reaching to the very end of her own tether and stretching her hand out for George.

'Grab on!' she yelled, as George's pace started to slow. 'George? George?'

'I'm ... fine ...' panted George, just a few metres away from her. 'Just ... a ... little ...'

Vi watched in horror as George's hand

suddenly slumped off the controller.

'George?' she cried. 'George!'

'DAD!' Russell screamed from *Spiderling*. 'DAD! WAKE UP!'

It was no use. George Sprout was unconscious.

Vi tugged at her tether to gain the few centimetres she needed to reach him. Straining every muscle in her body, she willed her arms to grow the tiny distance they needed to pull George back into them. She yanked and yanked at the tether, but there was no more give. She reached out for him once more, splaying her fingers to their furthest possible length. But it was no good.

George Sprout was out of her reach.

And he was drifting off into space.

CHAPTER 8

'**G**ive me that . . . Vi! Vi! You need to get back here, right now!'

Vi heard her father's voice, but was unable to find her own. She watched George floating away into space, like a lost kite in a gentle breeze.

'Can you hear me? Vi? Are you OK?' Robert yelled into her ear. 'Vi! VI!'

But Vi still had no words. She could only watch as the man she'd first met as her teacher, Mr Sprout, but grown to love as her nearly-stepdad, George, drifted away to certain death.

'Dad?' came Russell's quiet voice over the headset. 'Dad? Dad, do you copy?'

Vi heard a rustling and the muffled sound of her mum's tearful voice.

'It's OK, Russ,' Easter sobbed. 'We're going to be OK.'

'Vi!' her dad shouted again. 'I don't know if you can hear me, but we're winching you in. Just hang on – we're getting you back.'

Vi tried to form the words, but nothing came. George was gone.

She felt a tug on her suit and her body being forced backwards, as the tether pulled her towards *Spiderling*. The distance between her and George arced out in front of her as it grew bigger. She just couldn't believe it. George had dreamt of going to space. And now he'd never leave. Maybe there'd be some comfort in that one day.

But not today.

She surrendered her body to the tether as she was dragged ever closer to the airlock. If only George had listened. If only he'd stayed away from that stupid jetpack.

Two memories flashed across her mind in the same instant.

Know who needs saving, came her nan's voice in the hospital.

I'm being a hero, came George's as he'd launched his jetpack.

His jetpack.

The jetpack that was identical to the one on Vi's suit.

Vi knew that if she thought about it for more than two seconds, she would realize what a stupid thing she was about to do. But then, Vi figured, most of the things she'd done lately were pretty stupid.

And, besides, when did she ever think about anything for more than two seconds?

She reached down to the button that would release her from the tether.

'Nearly there, baby,' came her father's soothing voice. 'We've got you.'

'Sorry, Dad,' said Vi, as she looked down at the tether and the safety it guaranteed. 'But I have to go and get our George.'

She pushed the button and felt herself disconnect from the tether. She copied exactly what George had done to locate the joystick beneath the arm of her suit.

'Here goes,' she said to herself and pushed the joystick. Her body immediately surged forward with the power of the jetpack. Like George had been, she was a bit wobbly at first. But within a few tries, she had control.

'VALENTINE DAY!' came her father's roar. 'What the— Reconnect this instant!'

'Dad, chill,' said Vi as she pushed the controller harder and felt a surge of acceleration propelling her through the airless darkness towards George. A heady cocktail of fear and adrenaline surged through her veins. She was gaining on him.

'Rod? Russell?' she called into her headset.

'Vi?' Russell called back. 'Vi, I can't believe you are— I don't know how to—'

'I need to know how to fix your dad's suit,' she said. 'He's been unconscious for too long.'

'Roger that,' said Russell, clearing his throat and adopting his professional techie voice again. 'According to the schematics, there is a manual repressurizing switch on his arm, near the elbow. Can you see it?'

'One second,' said Vi, as she finally caught up to George's floating body.

'Did you say the left side?'

'Right,' said Russell.

'Which one?' said Vi.

'The left is right,' Russell insisted.

'My right or your right?' Vi barked.

'For goodness' sake, what are they teaching you in schools these days?' came Rod's impatient growl. 'The switch is on the left side, just by his elbow.'

'That was all I needed to know,' grumbled Vi, immediately locating the switch and flipping it to the 'on' position. She watched George's suit bubble and wriggle.

'Come on, George, wake up!' she urged. 'It's OK, I've got you.'

She stared at George, willing him to come to, trying not to look at how far they both now were from *Spiderling*.

'George?' she called again. 'George!'

'Did you know,' mumbled George Sprout, as the pressure returned to his suit and the consciousness to his soul, 'that you could fit 1.3 million Earths into the sun?'

Vi watched as George Sprout regained his bearings and once again took control of his body and his space suit.

'Dad!' Russell cried again, joyfully this time. 'Dad! It's OK! Vi saved you!'

'Not yet I haven't,' said Vi grimly, turning herself around. 'Are you OK to fly back to *Spiderling*?'

'Come fly with me,' said a smiling George, blasting himself forward with his jetpack.

Vi smiled. She had to hand it to the man. He had some good lines.

They blasted together across the vast expanse, Earth glowing beneath them. Now that safety was in sight, Vi had to admit that this was one of the coolest things she'd ever done.

'Isn't it beautiful?' George said in awe.

'It really is,' said Vi, inwardly vowing to do more to care for her stunning planet if she were ever able to return to it.

The airlock opened up invitingly ahead. She was nearly there. She'd nearly done it. She—

In a moment's lapse of concentration, Vi wobbled on her joystick, sending her banging into the side of *Spiderling*. She suddenly felt a horrible rip as she bumped up against the jagged edges of the space station.

'Oh, no!' she cried as her suit started to sound all manner of alarms.

'*SUIT COMPROMISED*,' it unhelpfully informed her. '*CRITICAL FAILURE IMMINENT.*'

'Mayday! Mayday!' she cried out. 'I have a

tear in my suit!'

'Stay calm,' said George, gripping on to her and dragging her into the airlock before hitting the button to close the doors. 'Thirty seconds and you'll be OK. Just stay calm.'

The main doors to *Spiderling* took what seemed an eternity to close. The moment they made contact with one another, the timer started to tick down.

'Come on, come on!' Vi tried not to scream as the various functions of her suit started to fail in turn.

'*SUIT PRESSURE: FAIL; SUIT BATTERY: FAIL; SUIT OXYGEN: FAIL.*'

The suit continued to reel off the list of ways it was trying to kill her. Vi started panting in her panic.

'Get this thing off me!' she screamed, starting to tear at her helmet.

'Vi – NO!' George shouted, holding down her arms. 'Now listen to me. I need you to take a deep breath. In . . . twenty-three seconds, those doors are going to open and we are going to rip this suit straight off you. Are you standing by in there?'

'We're ready?' Vi heard her mum say, a telling

tremble in her voice.

'Darling, it's going to be OK,' Robert reassured her. 'We're here. We're all here.'

Vi looked at the reassuring face of George Sprout, who was smiling kindly at her.

'Just hold that breath,' he said. 'We're nearly done.'

Vi tried to steady herself and took a long, deep breath.

'Good girl,' beamed George, moving her as close to the doors as was possible without going through them. She looked at the countdown as her suit continued to scream warnings at her. *Fifteen seconds . . .*

'Did you know,' George said softly, 'the world record for holding a breath is over twenty-four minutes?'

She shook her head, terrified to let even the slightest wisp of air out of her body.

'I often wondered if they trained in the boys' toilets at school,' George mused. 'You need to hold your breath in there if you want to survive.'

Nine seconds.

Vi knew she held her breath for longer than this in the bath. But now her life was in the balance, these were the longest few seconds of her twelve years on the planet.

'Nearly there, sweetie,' said George, looking at the doors as if he too were willing them open. 'You ready in there? I'm going to push her through head first so you can take off her helmet.'

'Roger that,' came Robert's voice.

Five seconds. Vi's lungs were on fire; she didn't know how much longer she could hold it.

'I'm just going to lift you up,' said George. 'And you're going to be out of here in three . . . two . . . one . . .'

Vi heard the doors spring open and then was completely disorientated as a frantic blur of hands and voices surrounded her. She could hear the clasps of her helmet being opened – she was so desperate for the oxygen she knew was now pumping around *Spiderling* again.

'There you go, baby,' came her mum's relieved voice as the helmet was yanked from her sweaty head. 'You just take some long, deep breaths. It's OK, you're safe.'

Vi didn't need to be asked twice. As the rest of her family worked to free her and George from their suits, she gasped in the air that her lungs were crying out for. She felt her body being pulled from the suit – that felt good – and slowly, slowly, every muscle inside her started to unclench and relax.

She looked at her mum, who was clasping her hand and stroking her hair.

'My Vi,' she whispered. 'My brilliant Vi.'

Vi turned her body the right way up, to see George floating just across from her, his son in his arms, a grateful grin on his face. They charged towards one another into a massive flying hug.

'Thank you, Vi,' sobbed George. 'Thank you so much.'

They hovered there for a moment, the sheer relief of being alive flowing gratefully between them.

Vi looked over George's shoulder at Russell, who smiled back at her, before propelling himself over to her for his own huge hug. She'd lived with Russell for over a year now. But she wasn't sure they'd ever hugged before. It felt kinda . . . nice.

'I don't know what to say,' he said. 'Thank you.'

'That works,' she said. And she meant it. Besides, after all their adventures, she owed Russell one. Several, actually.

She felt her father's strong arms pull her away from Russell's and into his.

'Don't you ever put yourself in danger like that again!' he ordered. 'Thank everything you're OK.'

'She's amazing,' said George, taking Russell back into his arms.

'She is,' spat Robert. 'No thanks to you!'

'Robert!' Easter shouted. 'Now is not the time!'

'He nearly got our child killed!' Robert shouted.

'Dad!' Vi shouted back. 'George didn't do anything, I chose to go after him.'

'And you did a great job, kid,' said Rod, silencing Robert with a single look. Vi heard her father muttering angrily into her hair.

'Nice one, Vi,' grinned her nan, as Ted floated behind her amiably with a big bruise already shining on his head. 'Now I've got some lovely cottage pie rehydrating. Why don't we all have a bite to eat?'

Vi didn't think she could eat a thing, she still had so much adrenaline pumping through her body. She watched as George approached her dad.

'Robert,' said George quietly. 'I had no idea Vi would do what she did – I would never, ever put her in any danger, I love her—'

'Don't you speak to me,' Robert hissed back. 'If it were up to me, you'd still be floating around out there like a lost balloon and I'd have all the nails left on my fingers. Stay out of my way. She's my daughter. And I'll be the one protecting her from now on.'

Robert floated away as aggressively as the microgravity environment would allow. Vi swam over to a deflated George.

'Sorry about my dad,' she whispered. 'He's just . . .'

'You don't have to explain.' George smiled weakly. 'I get it. He loves you so much. He's just looking out for you. I'd probably be the same.'

'No, you wouldn't,' Vi said, squeezing his arm. 'You love me differently. And that's why I'm so lucky to have you two. I get to be loved both ways.'

'Oh, Vi,' said George, taking her into a hug again. 'You are such a special girl.'

'Says the man who once gave me four out of ten on a geography test,' Vi reminded him.

'You did confuse Norwich with Norway,' said George. 'Although did you know that Norwich was the first place in the UK to use postcodes, so . . .'

Vi laughed and pulled her nearly-stepdad beside her.

'Come on,' she smiled. 'We wouldn't want to let the cottage pie dehydrate.'

CHAPTER 9

Sometime later – it was hard to tell day from night in space – Vi had finally got some much-needed sleep, *Moonbreaker* was safely refuelled and the family was getting ready to leave *Spiderling* and Ted.

'Well, I'm going to miss having you all around the place,' said Ted as they prepared to board their shuttle. 'It's been ever so lovely having the company.'

'I'm just sorry we can't take you with us,' Vi said. 'We're a bit short of seats.'

'Oh, it's no bother,' said Ted, waving the thought away with a hand. 'I'm perfectly happy here until someone can give me a lift – and you've got important work to do. But if you pass this way again, be sure to pop in and see me. I've got plenty more space ice cream I've been saving for special.'

'Thanks, Logan,' said Rod, shaking Ted's hand. 'We'll probably die horribly in the course of this mission. But grateful for the invitation anyways.'

'Oh, you are a card!' laughed Ted, punching Rod's arm and then immediately regretting it. 'You be on your way – the world won't save itself, you know!'

'Thanks, Ted – for everything,' Vi said, giving him a hug. 'And . . . it does all work out for Ross and Rachel. So don't worry.'

'Oh, how marvellous!' said Ted, a small tear coming to his eye. 'I had a good feeling about those two. See you soon, I hope. Safe travels.'

'See ya, Ted,' said Russell as the airlock doors closed, before releasing them again to take their seats on *Moonbreaker*.

'I just don't get it,' said Vi. 'How can he be happy up there all by himself?'

'Not everyone needs saving,' repeated Indy, strapping her seat belt. 'He's made a life for himself up there. One he likes. You can't ask for much more.'

'He could ask for the next series of *Friends*,' muttered Vi, as Russell skilfully manoeuvred

Moonbreaker away from the landing pad.

'Nicely done, Sprout Junior,' said Rod admiringly as they disengaged from the space station.

'Thanks,' said Russell shyly, hitching his glasses up his nose.

'Better than your father's effort,' muttered Robert.

'Go knot your tie,' George muttered back.

'That's the funny thing about life,' Nan mused. 'You don't often get the one you thought you wanted. I was planning to be a teacher.'

'You were?' Vi queried. She'd never known that about her nan.

'I was,' Nan smiled. 'But while I was studying, I broke a few records with my maths scores. Got the tap on the shoulder from SPIDER and that was that. That's the thing. I didn't get the life I thought I wanted. But, by gumbo, I got the one I needed.'

She grinned at Vi, who tried to grin back. She'd never really talked to Nan about her life. She'd always seen Nan as . . . Nan. But she had a whole life before being a mother and a grandmother that Vi knew nothing about. One she wanted to know more about. One she didn't know if she'd have time to find out about.

Vi shook her head. She wasn't going to think like that. She was going to save Indy and then they'd have all the time in the world. Just like they should have.

'Next stop – NIDUS!' Rod announced, as *Moonbreaker* accelerated away from *Spiderling* and back out into deep space.

'What do you think Umbra is doing now?' Vi asked Easter, who'd been reluctant to let her go since her spacewalk adventure.

'Who knows?' Easter sighed. 'I don't know anything about Honey any more.'

'Now I think on it,' Nan added, 'there was always something a bit off about that one. Never could quite put my finger on it. But she was your friend, so I didn't like to say anything.'

'I wish you had,' said Easter quietly, turning her gaze out of the window.

A short while passed. Vi had been so caught up in Umbra as a villain, she realized she hadn't considered that she was also her mum's best friend, practically part of their family. Yes, Easter was a world-beating spy. But she was also a human being. And her arch-enemy had been hiding beneath her nose as her BFF all these years. If Vi knew her mum, she'd be feeling that horrible combination of stupid and guilty that Vi knew all too well from when she messed up. Much as Easter hated Umbra, she'd loved Honey B. That must be a very confusing mix.

'What will you . . . do to her?' Vi asked. 'You know, when we find her?'

Easter turned and looked at her daughter.

'We have a world to save,' she replied grimly. 'I'll do whatever's necessary.'

'Well said,' muttered Indy quietly. Vi hadn't known her nan was still listening. She suspected Indy listened to a lot more than Vi realized.

'So now that we're fully fuelled and on course,' Russell announced, 'we should arrive at NIDUS no later than—'

BANG!

Moonbreaker and its entire crew were rocked by a sudden and almighty crash.

'What was that?!' Vi cried.

'An asteroid?' George suggested. 'Some space debris, I think?'

'Think again,' said Rod as a huge and familiar space shuttle suddenly rose up in front of them. Vi had only seen it once before, but that was enough to cement it in her brain. It was white with a black nose and wing tips. It had the word *Spinneret* emblazoned across its hull. And it had a deeply unwelcome face at its helm.

'Umbra!' said the family in unison.

'Now, this is awkward,' came Honey B's voice into their shuttle, her face glowering from her control deck. 'I thought I'd made it quite clear that our friendship was over.'

Vi looked at her former godmother. Honey B was sweet, ditzy, clutzy. But as Umbra, she was totally different. Cold. Deadly.

'She's accessed our comms frequency,' whispered Rod, frantically jabbing the console. 'Keep her talking.'

'We were never friends,' Easter replied grimly. 'I was friends with Honey, not you. And I'm coming for you, Umbra.'

'Oh, Easter – it's always the same with you, isn't it?' Umbra sniffed, wiping her nose with a tissue. 'You're just that little bit behind. You're too late. Your ship can't hack it.'

'Oh, yeah?' Rod challenged. '*Moonbreaker* is twice the shuttle that *Spinneret* ever was.'

'Not with all that damage,' Umbra tutted.

'Pah,' spat Rod. 'What damage?'

'This damage,' said Umbra, a whole artillery of guns suddenly appearing out of small hatches on the front of *Spinneret*. 'Maybe this time you'll take the hint.'

And with a twisted grin, Umbra unleashed a flurry of laser power on *Moonbreaker*. Vi could feel their rocket being battered by the relentless volley of shots Honey was firing at them. They were sitting ducks. There was no way *Moonbreaker* could stand this for long.

'Rod! Is this thing armed?' Robert shouted over the noise of the shots.

'Whaddya think?' Rod growled back, flipping a switch to reveal dozens of gun barrels all around *Moonbreaker*'s exterior.

'Shall I open fire?' George offered.

'I think this one is more Robert's department,' said Rod, hitting a button and raising a controller in front of Robert's seat. 'You ready, Ford?'

'Oh, yes,' said Robert, worryingly comfortable with a destructive weapon in his hands, Vi observed.

'Then – ATTACK!' Rod commanded, a second after Robert had already opened fire on the *Spinneret*.

'You'd better get me one of those too,' said Easter, dropping Vi's hand and going immediately into spy mode.

'Me and all,' said Nan, rubbing her hands with glee.

'The more the merrier,' Rod replied, bringing more controllers up in front of Easter and Indy's chairs. 'Ladies . . .'

'Can I have one?' Vi asked.

'NO!' said all the adults at once, forcing her to sulk back in her seat.

'Come on, Sprout Junior – let's get out of here,' said Rod, urging new pilot Russell to push a huge lever forward, sending *Moonbreaker* into a massive acceleration. Vi was forced back in her seat at the sudden thrust of speed as Russell sped away from Umbra's attack.

'YEE-HAH!' Rod cried as *Moonbreaker* blasted through space, Umbra giving chase behind them.

'TAKE THAT!' Nan whooped as she spun around in her seat and fired gleefully at Umbra. For someone whose clock was ticking down, Vi had to admit, Indy really was having the time of her life.

Vi looked anxiously out of the window. *Moonbreaker* was the superior rocket to *Spinneret*, no doubt. They were pulling away with every second. But Umbra wasn't giving up easily.

'She can still hit us from this range,' Robert said, focusing on his target through the cross hairs. 'You need to change course.'

'Negative,' said George. 'Continue on course, Russ. A straight line gives us maximum speed. There is . . . something . . . up ahead, a planet, a moon – something. If we get past it, *Spinneret* will get caught in its orbit; it doesn't have our thrust.'

'Her weaponry is outdated and can only fire in one angle,' Robert insisted. 'If we change course, her guns can't touch us.'

'If we get further away, her guns won't touch us anyway,' said George, staring intently ahead. 'We're approaching the moon in under thirty seconds.'

'We might not have thirty seconds!' Robert cried as *Moonbreaker* took another massive hit, shaking the shuttle to its core.

'EAT LASER, UMBRA!' Nan shouted, whooping and spinning around so quickly on her chair, she nearly fell off it.

'I'm telling you, Umbra is gaining,' said Robert

as another laser pounded *Moonbreaker*. 'We can't take much more of this. We need to change course.'

'Unidentified mass approaching in T-minus fifteen seconds,' Russell announced, looking to Rod for guidance.

'I'm telling you,' George insisted. 'She will get sucked into its orbit.'

'You sure about that, Sprout?' asked Rod. Even he was looking concerned. Or as concerned as Rod Staff ever looked.

'YES!' George cried defensively. 'It's just basic maths. We have the superior thrust boosters. We'll be fine.'

Another almighty blast shook *Moonbreaker*.

'*WARNING*,' *Moonbreaker*'s computer announced. '*THRUST BOOSTERS DISABLED. ORBITAL PULL ENGAGED. BRACE FOR IMPACT.*'

The *Moonbreaker* slowed to a terrifying halt. They weren't racing now – they were falling.

'Have fun,' Umbra laughed from her ship as she backed away. 'I hope you don't mind – I warmed the locals up a little for you. Hope you enjoy their welcome.'

'What does she mean by that?' Vi asked.

'Who knows?' Easter sighed, releasing her controller and grabbing Vi's hand. 'We've got bigger problems right now.'

'You IDIOT!' Robert yelled at George. 'Basic maths? We're going to crash!'

'But . . . I don't understand . . . This doesn't make any sense,' George stammered.

The *Spinneret* blasted away, leaving *Moonbreaker* being dragged towards the moon beneath.

'Rod!' Easter demanded in her agent voice. 'What is the evacuation protocol?'

'There isn't one,' Rod growled. 'I designed *Moonbreaker* to withstand any conceivable impact. We're safest here. We'll live. Probably.'

Vi really wanted to believe Rod. But as they were dragged through the planet's atmosphere and towards the surface below, she had her doubts.

An ashen George turned to Easter.

'I'm so sorry,' he said to her. 'I thought—'

'You didn't think at all!' Robert yelled. 'You've lived your life in books! I've lived mine in the real world! And in the real world, in a real battle, you don't rely on "basic maths", you moron!'

'It's OK, Dad,' said Russell weakly. 'If Rod says we're going to be OK, we're going to be OK.'

'I never said you were going to be OK,' said Rod as *Moonbreaker* spun towards the green mass below. 'I said you'd probably live. But it's going to be a bumpy landing. Everyone, brace yourselves . . .'

The ground was coming towards them at terrifying speed. Vi felt Easter's hand find hers again as they fell through the sky and into a thick forest, the tall trees whipping *Moonbreaker* as it tore through their canopy. The space shuttle was tossed this way and that by the thick branches, which battered the beleaguered vessel from one side to the other.

'Here it comes!' Rod warned. 'Prepare for impact in three . . . two . . .'

But if Rod made it to one, Vi didn't hear it.

Because *Moonbreaker* had already smashed into the ground below.

'Sir! Sir! I think I've got them!'

The Wolf raced over to Agent Money's station.

'Got who?' he demanded.

'Well, everyone,' Agent Money blushed. 'One of my training rotations at SPIDER was in the tech lab with Agent Unicorn — I mean, Umbra — when she was developing her edible tracking dye.'

The Wolf allowed his lips to consider the suggestion of a smile. Of course — the edible tracking dye. Honey B had laced the food at SPIDER HQ and the buffet at Easter's second wedding with it. It was how Umbra had found The Wolf and captured him and his sister Charlie. It was how she'd tracked Robert and blown up his house. It was how — Isaac thought with an uncomfortable lump in his throat — Umbra had located and murdered The Cardinal. That dye had caused no end of trouble. Could it now help them to find her?

'The signal's very weak,' Agent Money continued, pulling up a screen with some faint dots scattered across it. 'But I'm sure it's them.'

'What's that one?' The Wolf asked, pointing to a lone flashing dot moving across the screen at some speed.

'That's Agent Unicorn, I mean, Umbra,' Agent Money explained. The Wolf smiled. Honey had eaten her own spiked food. They had her. Served her right.

'She's on course for NIDUS and should arrive there within hours,' Money continued.

The Wolf cursed under his breath.

'And these here?' he asked, pointing to a cluster of still dots in the bottom corner.

'That's Agents Lynx, Labyrinth and Redback, Sir Charge — I mean, Robert Ford — and the children. I forget their names . . .'

'Why aren't they flashing?'

'The edible tracking dye detects movement, sir,' said Agent Money softly. 'If the dots aren't flashing, the subjects aren't moving. They might be asleep. Or it could mean . . .'

The Wolf looked at the lifeless dots on the screen. There was no way Easter would be asleep while Umbra was on the loose. He willed the dots to move. But they just stayed there. Horribly still.

'Where are they?' he asked.

'We're unsure,' said Agent Money, pulling up a map of the solar system. 'Our mapping of space is still somewhat inaccurate and incomplete. They appear to be on an uncharted moon. I'm working on establishing a more precise location and re-establishing contact.'

The Wolf looked proudly at Agent Money.

'Fantastic work, agent,' he said – and he meant it.

'Thank you, sir,' said Agent Money modestly.

'Now get back to work,' said The Wolf gruffly. He didn't need his junior agents thinking he was going soft. 'Send me those coordinates the moment you have them—'

'Everyone, cease and desist whatever you are doing!' came a commanding bark, followed by the sound of synchronized footsteps. 'Immediately!'

The Wolf released an exhausted sigh. Now what?

'What are you doing?' he demanded, turning to face the general and his small battalion of troops. 'How dare you interrupt my mission at this critical time?'

The general marched over and handed The Wolf a piece of paper.

'It's not *your* mission any more,' he said smugly. 'I'm relieving you of your command.'

'On whose authority?' The Wolf asked, although he already knew the answer.

'I told you I was going to the top,' General Bark

replied. 'I went to Old Lady. And she's not swallowing any of this.'

Isaac Payne ripped open the letter that confirmed he was to stand down and give the general control of his mission. The Wolf had trained as a military man and knew how to follow an order. He knew that he was exhausted, had friends up there and perhaps didn't have the objectivity he needed to make the tough calls.

But he also knew that the general was still an almighty butthead.

'You are to order your people to follow my command and do exactly as I say,' the general continued.

Agent Money stood up, unfortunately forgetting that she was still attached to her station by her headphones. After a moment's struggle with the wiring, she collected herself and stood firmly up to the general.

'I only take orders from Agent Wolf,' she said bravely. The Wolf was impressed – he had seriously underestimated this kid. Even if she did have her shoes on the wrong feet. The General took a few menacing steps, until he was right in Agent Money's face.

'You will follow my orders, or you will be relieved from your post,' he snarled.

Agent Money gulped slightly, but stood her ground.

'Like I said,' she said quietly. 'I take my orders from Agent Wolf.'

'Then you are to stand down immediately,' said the general, summoning one of his troops to take Money's place. 'What were you working on?'

'Just a hunch,' said Agent Money, switching off her screen. 'I was following a lead using some old tech we developed at SPIDER. But ...'

Agent Money looked over at The Wolf, who gave her an imperceptible nod.

'But ... it didn't work,' Agent Money said more confidently. 'I've wiped it from my hard drive.'

The Wolf allowed himself an internal smile. Money was proving valuable.

'Insubordinate AND ineffectual!' the general snapped. 'Good riddance. I will deal with you later – but for now, GET OUT OF MY SIGHT!'

Agent Money nearly leapt out of her skin at the general's sudden volume, but allowed her replacement to take his place at her station.

'And you can get out of here too,' the general

growled at The Wolf. 'Some of us have work to do.'

The general turned on his heel and marched to the centre of the room.

'We need a precise location for Umbra and the firepower to blow her out of the sky,' said the general. 'I want updates from every section NOW!'

The Wolf watched as the general assumed command of his mission. He'd met men like the general many times before. And he knew how dangerous they could be.

But for now, all the fight had gone out of him. It was time to stand aside.

Or was it?

'Sir,' Agent Money whispered, gesturing for The Wolf to follow her to a quieter part of the room. He followed until they were out of earshot.

'What?' he asked. Agent Money pulled out her phone.

'I downloaded the tracking information on to my phone before wiping my computer,' she said excitedly, showing The Wolf the screen. 'Look.'

The Wolf took her phone. Umbra was still flashing across space. He should really share this information with the general.

But then something else caught his eye.

One of the previously still dots had started to flash. And then another. And then a third. Within moments, the whole cluster was flashing on the screen.

'They're alive!' he whispered to Agent Money.

'It would appear so, sir,' Agent Money grinned back.

That was all Isaac needed to hear. Feeling a renewed burst of energy, The Wolf strode back into the control centre.

'What are you still doing here?' the general said unpleasantly.

'SPIDER protocol dictates that a senior agent must be present at any deployment of SPIDER staff,' said The Wolf, thinking warmly of his late predecessor, Walter Toppington, AKA The Cardinal. 'You know perfectly well that I can't leave. Or would you like me to check with Old Lady? You know she'd eat you alive.'

The Wolf enjoyed watching the general squirm with irritation. They both knew The Wolf was right. But it was fun to watch him struggle.

'Stay where I can see you,' the general snapped.

'And that's an order!'

'Understood,' said The Wolf, and he meant it.

Because while Easter and her family were still in the game, Isaac Payne wasn't going anywhere.

CHAPTER 10

'**O**uch.'

    Vi's hand went groggily to her head. Was she alive? She figured that the fact she was asking the question was probably a good sign.

The last few moments before her consciousness was pummelled out of her came piling into her brain in a confused lump. She'd been in space ... hadn't she? Or had she dreamt it? A quick squint out of the window suggested she wasn't there now – there were trees everywhere, inside *Moonbreaker* and out. Had the family made it home?

Family.

Her family.

Oh, no.

'Hey!' she shouted, throwing a tree branch off her lap. 'Hey! Anyone there?'

'Valentine?' came Robert's groggy response. 'Vi – are you OK?'

Vi followed the sound of her father's voice to another pile of foliage. She yanked it off him and found Robert beneath – bruised and bleeding, but very much alive.

'Quick,' she said, helping him out of his seat. 'We need to find the others.'

They made their way quickly around *Moonbreaker*'s crew capsule, pulling the tree branches and crash detritus away to uncover their semi-conscious family members.

'Nan!' said Vi, discovering Nan slumped over her gun control. 'Nan! Are you all right?'

A wave of nausea passed over her. Vi wasn't sure if it was concussion or fear. Was Nan . . .

'Nan!' she shouted, shaking Indy roughly. 'Nan! Wake up!'

'All right, all right – hold yer horses,' Indy finally muttered, replacing her wonky glasses squarely back on her face. 'Give a girl a minute.'

Vi let out a massively relieved sigh and threw her arms around her beloved grandmother, who chuckled softly in response.

'Don't you worry about me, love,' she said into

Vi's hair. 'They built me to last.'

Vi felt another wave of nausea rise up in her throat. If only that were true.

But she immediately corrected herself. It *was* true. And if it wasn't, she was going to find a way to make it true. Although first, she had some other people to save . . .

Vi continued to make her way around the deck rousing Easter, Russell, Rod and George to full consciousness.

'Everyone OK?' Rod growled.

'Sound as a pound,' said Indy brightly. 'That shook out the cobwebs. I could murder a cuppa, though.'

Vi looked around at what remained of *Moonbreaker*. It wasn't just the cobwebs that had been shaken out by their crash landing. The rocket was a mess – the glass screens were shattered and assorted switches and dials were hanging by their springs.

'It's only superficial,' said Rod, as if reading her mind. 'I've got everything we need to fix her in the back. Few hours, we'll be out of here.'

'Where are we?' Russell asked.

'I've no idea,' said George. 'I was trying to find

out before we crashed.'

'Before you *made* us crash,' snapped Robert.

'I think we're on a moon, but not one I'm aware of,' George said. 'The good news is, the atmosphere has the same composition as Earth's, so we can breathe the air.'

'How do you know?' said Robert suspiciously.

George pointed to the smashed windows around the spacecraft.

'Because we're not dead.'

Russell snorted at his dad's deadpan. Robert rolled his eyes and straightened his tie.

'Right, I'm going to get started on these repairs,' said Rod, disengaging his mobility scooter. 'Lotus Flower, care to lend a hand?'

'Sure,' said Nan brightly. 'Go on, you young scamps. Go and get some fresh air. Stretch your legs.'

'Are you sure?' Vi asked. 'I'm happy to stay with you.'

'Nah,' scoffed her nan. 'You go. I could do with the peace and quiet.'

'And I could do with a long kiss from those sweet lips,' growled Rod.

That was all Vi needed to hear. She quickly

got up and made her way hastily to *Moonbreaker*'s exit hatch. Delighted as she was that Nan was OK, the thought of her grandmother having a great big snog with Rod was enough to prompt another massive wave of nausea.

She followed Easter out of the hatch and was grateful for the burst of fresh air that greeted her. She realized she'd spent the past few hours – days, perhaps – without any real air and she quietly promised never to take that luxury for granted again should she return to Earth. She glanced back at *Moonbreaker* from the outside. It looked like Rod was right. Although she was a mess inside, the exterior of the ship had sustained very little damage, so Vi felt confident that Rod could indeed fix them up and have them on their way before too long.

'I really need to pee,' said Russell, running off into a nearby thicket.

'Me too,' George agreed.

'Me three,' said Robert, racing off behind them.

'Quite the adventure we're having,' said Easter, coming and putting her arm around Vi's shoulder.

'For a change,' said Vi, making her mum smile.

'Maybe next year, we could just go caravanning? Like a normal family.'

Easter laughed and nuzzled into Vi's ear.

'I don't think there's ever going to be anything normal about our family,' she said.

Vi had to agree. And she wouldn't really have it any other way.

'How are you holding up?' Easter asked.

'I'm all right,' said Vi honestly. 'How are you?'

Easter looked surprised to be asked the question.

'I'm . . . I've got a lot on my mind,' she said – and Vi sensed that was honest too.

'Well, if I can help you, you only have to ask,' Vi replied. Watching Easter care for Indy had made her realize that even mums needed a bit of support sometimes.

'I appreciate that,' said Easter, pulling Vi in for a big and very welcome hug.

After a few lovely moments in her mum's embrace, Vi extricated herself from Easter's arms and took a good look around. They were in a forest, one that could have been any of the ones Vi had visited back on Earth. The tall trees that surrounded them made it hard to see anything beyond their immediate vicinity, but there was nothing to suggest anything particularly out of the ordinary about this new place.

'I wonder if anyone lives here?' Vi asked.

'I doubt it,' said Easter. 'If other intelligent life forms existed in space, I'm sure they would have made contact by now. Extraterrestrial life forms are a fascinating fantasy. But I think the reality is, we are in this big, wide universe all alone.'

'Um . . . Easter,' came Robert's voice behind them. 'Slight situation, here.'

'No. Way,' huffed Easter. 'We picked up toilet paper from *Spiderling* – go and get it yourself.'

'I think it'll take more than loo roll to sort this one out, dear heart,' said Robert.

'For heaven's sake, can't you do the simplest— Oh.'

Vi turned around to see what had interrupted her mother. It was rare that something was able to.

But that wasn't the only unusual thing facing Vi in that moment.

For one thing, Robert, George and Russell were all standing in front of them with their hands in the air and their trousers around their ankles.

And for another, a grey, bald-headed alien was

holding them at ray-gun point.

Vi felt her jaw slacken and her mind question her eyesight. What the— Aliens? They existed? But how . . .

She took her last thought back. There was something very out of the ordinary about this place.

The alien turned to Vi and her mum and pointed its ray gun towards them.

'I guess we're not so alone after all,' Easter whispered to Vi, as they both slowly raised their hands.

'Where are you taking us?' Robert asked for the millionth time as the alien continued to route-march them through the forest with their hands tied behind their backs.

Vi saw the alien look around. While at first the very presence of an extraterrestrial had been a big shock, as they'd walked, she'd been watching their captor closely. On closer inspection, the alien didn't seem so terrifying after all. If anything, it seemed . . . nervous.

'It clearly doesn't understand us,' said George irritably. 'So why not save your voice?'

'At least I can save something,' Robert snapped back, as the alien jabbed its ray gun into his back. 'This is all thanks to you.'

'I believe you were the one who launched us into space in the first place,' George argued.

'And you were the one who messed up the landing at *Spiderling*,' Robert shot back.

'I was not!' George argued.

'Yes, you were!'

'Wasn't!'

'Was!'

'Wasn't!'

'Was!'

'WILL YOU BOTH BE QUIET!' Easter shouted, in the absence of Indy to do it for her. Vi hoped that Rod and Indy were OK aboard *Moonbreaker*. The alien had briefly examined the ship, but clearly hadn't discovered them. No doubt Rod had a panic room on his space shuttle. He had seventeen of them back at Ragnarok. Besides, it wasn't Rod and Indy they needed to worry about right now. It was themselves.

'Please,' George asked the alien. 'Can you

understand us? Can you tell us where we are?'

The alien stopped and looked around again. It looked like it was considering something. Finally, it pulled a . . . thing that looked like a silver jelly bean out of its pocket. It offered it to George.

'What's this?' George asked. 'Is it a pill? Do I swallow it?'

He opened his mouth to eat it, but the alien gestured frantically to stop him. Approaching with extreme caution, the alien started to gingerly move the jelly bean towards George's head.

'Be careful, darling,' said Easter nervously.

'It's probably some brain-eating device,' Robert said unhelpfully. 'Although it's going to go hungry in your head.'

'Dad,' said Russell cautiously as the alien leant towards George's ear. 'Do you think that's a good idea?'

'It's OK,' said George, smiling at the alien. 'I think . . . I think it's friendly.'

'A friendly brain-sucker,' muttered Robert, as the alien pointed its gun back at him. 'They're the best sort.'

George shook his head to settle the jelly bean in his ear. There was a nervous silence as they all waited to see what the device would do to him. Vi's mind raced through countless possibilities. Would it make his head explode? Would it melt him from the inside? Would it transform him into a monster?

'Oh . . . hello!' George finally said. 'Yes, nice to meet you. I'm George Sprout. Well, it's a pleasure to meet you too.'

'OK, he's finally cracked,' said Robert. 'He's talking to himself.'

'No – I'm talking to my friend here,' said George, as the alien removed more jelly beans from its white robe. 'This is a communication device. Take one in your ear – you can understand what they're saying.'

'No, thank you,' said Robert, headbutting the alien's hand away. 'I don't want to understand it.'

'Said every idiot ever,' said Easter, accepting a jelly bean in her ear, as did Russell and Vi. With her device in place, Vi was immediately able to tune into the conversation.

'. . . and so we communicate through telepathy in order to render our communication most efficient and effective,' the alien was halfway through explaining.

'Fascinating,' said George.

'Where are we?' Vi asked.

'You are on the moon of I-Dem,' the alien explained.

'I-Dem?' said George. 'I thought I knew all the moons in our solar system.'

'You'd be forgiven for knowing nothing of us,' the alien replied kindly. 'Our moon is surrounded by an invisibility field for our protection. From where have you travelled?'

'Earth,' Russell explained. 'And we'd really like to get back there. Can you let us go?'

'I'm afraid I cannot,' the alien explained. 'After a recent security breach, we are required to take all visitors to the Supreme Leaders, on pain of extermination. But on a personal note, I am thrilled to meet more of your kind.'

'More?' Easter asked quickly. 'There have been other humans here?'

'Just one,' said the alien, recoiling slightly. 'They stayed briefly, but left only devastation in their wake. They called themselves . . . Um Bra.'

'Umbra,' Vi and Easter repeated simultaneously.

'Umbra was here? On . . .'

'I-Dem,' the alien confirmed. 'Yes. But I cannot

speak more of it, the Supreme Leaders have forbidden it.'

'These Supreme Leaders sound fun,' Vi muttered.

'I am not familiar with this concept of "fun",' the alien repeated. 'But if it means "all-powerful and terrifying", then, yes, they are enormous fun. I am taking you to them now.'

'What will they do to us?' Easter asked cautiously.

'That would be for them to decide,' said the alien — sadly, Vi thought. 'I am merely a humble guard. Such things are beyond my meagre brain.'

'Well, you seem perfectly smart to me,' said George kindly. 'Thank you for answering our questions.'

'It is my pleasure,' said the alien. 'I hope I might have the opportunity to ask you some of my own. For now, we must cease communication. We are approaching the city and the Supreme Leaders have prohibited contact with other life forms after the dastardly machinations of Um Bra.'

Vi had so many more things she wanted to ask, but the alien had resumed the brisk march at ray-gun point and silence quickly fell upon their group again.

They soon came to a clearing, revealing the city that the alien had mentioned. Unsurprisingly for an alien planet, it was quite unlike anything Vi had ever seen. All the buildings, and there were thousands, were exactly the same colour – grey – and of the same construction – square with four windows and one door. The only difference was their size. This same building was in every conceivable size around the city, with the largest one atop the hill that supported them all. There was no greenery here, no other kind of building, nothing to break up the uniformity of the identical structures. It was . . . it was kind of boring to look at.

'Take. Me. To. Your. Leader,' Robert said loudly and slowly to their captor. Vi shook her head – it was the same as her dad's approach to every foreign language and equally as successful. The alien continued to say nothing, but directed them through the precise grid of the city's roads, straight towards the biggest building at its heart. As the family was paraded past the dwellings, creatures like their captor looked out of windows and moved aside in the street. Like the buildings, every one of them looked the same – grey skin, bald heads, white robes – their only difference was in their size. They stared at the newcomers as if . . . well, as if they were aliens. Which Vi quickly realized, to these individuals, they were.

Their guard finally brought them to the large building and hit on the door for access, which was quickly granted. Vi and her family were led through a succession of plain grey corridors until they came to a large, square hall. In the centre of the otherwise empty room were four identical, large grey chairs. And sitting in them were four identical bald, grey aliens.

Their guard bowed to the seated four.

'Greeting, Supreme Leaders,' they said. 'I came across these human intruders in the forest and have brought them here to you, as per your directive.'

'What were you doing in the forest, I–160407?' one of the Supreme Leaders demanded. 'You know it is forbidden.'

'I . . . er . . . was checking for more human intruders like Um Bra, Supreme Leader Two,' the alien replied. 'I was concerned for our planet's safety.'

'Our planet's safety is none of your concern!' a second alien barked. Vi now noticed a tiny purple badge on each of their white robes. 'Your tiny brain has no capacity for such matters. You will be disciplined for your transgression. We will deal with you later.'

'Yes, Supreme Ones,' said the alien sadly, stepping back to the grey doors. Vi couldn't help but feel a bit sorry for their captor. Even if they had tied them up and brought them to an alien city from which there was no obvious escape and had therefore put them in grave danger.

Actually, Vi didn't feel that sorry for them.

Vi looked around the vast, grey hall to see if they could make a run for it. But before the thought had fully crystallized, grey metal bands snaked up from the floor, wrapped around her feet and locked them to the spot. She was stuck. She turned her attention back to the Supreme Leaders.

'Why have you returned?' A third voice rang through her brain. 'We made it clear what your fate would be on I-Dem before your escape!'

'Answer Supreme Leader Three – what are you doing back here?' came another angry voice. 'To be caught in our tractor beams once was foolish. Twice suggests you are either returning to wreak more chaos or are merely incredibly stupid!'

'Tractor beams?' said George suddenly. 'You mean, you made us crash here?'

'We ensure that any foreign object in our orbit is brought to us for inspection,' said Supreme Leader Two. 'It is part of our safety protocol, which is vital to our—'

'Ha!' cried George at Robert. 'You see? It wasn't my fault! Stick that in your tie and twist it!'

'LET. US. GO!' Robert shouted again, ignoring George and fighting off another alien who was trying to force a translator into his ear.

'Dad – sssshhhh,' said Vi, straining to hear the voices in her ear. 'Can you hear me? Can you understand me?'

'Your universal translator is fully functional,' came the first voice. 'I will ask you one more time – why have you returned?'

'Returned?' said Russell. 'We've never been here before.'

'Lies!' came Supreme Leader One's voice. Vi was starting to be able to tell them apart. 'Not two solar phases ago, you arrived here in your metal bird, overcame us with your New Or Troll and left before we could bring you to justice, leaving a devastating plague in your wake.'

'Umbra used the Neurotrol?' Vi mused. 'And what plague?'

'That is what Supreme Leader One communicated,' said Supreme Leader Four. 'One temporal moment we were going about our business. The next, you had our entire city performing a torturous physical trial you called the Floss. You made your escape, and yet you are back to try again . . .'

'OK, Umbra might have been here,' Vi explained. 'But we're not her!'

'And yet you look identical,' said Supreme Leader One. 'Coincidence? I don't think so.'

Vi looked down the line of her family. How could anyone think they were all the same?

'Now listen here,' said Robert, who had finally accepted the translator. 'You've got the wrong end of the stick – none of us is Umbra, but we are trying to catch Umbra, so if you just let us go . . .'

'Which is exactly what Um Bra would say!' roared Supreme Leader Three. 'Clearly Um Bra has cloned themselves in an attempt to take over the mighty I-Dem civilization! Although I would still like to fully understand the intricacies of the Floss.'

'No, you really have got this wrong,' said Easter. 'Honey . . . Umbra . . .'

'You see?' said the third voice. 'Even you can't remember your own disguise! We see through you, Um Bra, and will not this time submit to your New Or Troll, nor the devastating nasal slime disease you left in your wake.'

'Why aren't your mouths moving?' Robert asked, as if this were in any way relevant.

'On I-Dem, we communicate primarily by thought,' said Supreme Leader One. 'This way, we can ensure that the right words reach the right ears. How careless it would be to put your words where anyone can see or hear them. The translators allow us to understand your senseless human babble. We have observed your planet for some time. It is fascinating in its simplicity.'

'I say!' said Robert, bristling.

'So . . . if you knew about us, why haven't you made contact?' Russell asked.

There was a multiple snorting that Vi took for laughter.

'Why would we?' Supreme Leader One

scoffed. 'We have extensively analysed your So Shall Me Dear and discovered that the greatest concern for humans is sharing images of their breakfast. We have nothing meaningful to discuss with such a basic species.'

'This is an outrage!' Robert roared. 'I demand that you free us at once!'

'This is impossible,' said Supreme Leader Four. 'Last time you were here, Um Bra, you controlled us all. You tried to make us all the same and deny I-Dem the vibrant diversity that we hold so dear.'

'With the greatest of respect,' George began, making a small bow, 'what is it you want with us, oh, great ones?'

'Suck-up,' said Robert under his breath.

'I like this one,' whispered Supreme Leader Two, not quite quietly enough. 'We must make sure we mark him somehow to distinguish him from the others. We shall dissect him last.'

'DISSECT?' the whole family said at once.

'You escaped us once,' said the first voice. 'Before we had a chance to research your under-developed and flawed human form. I-Dem is a scientific civilization and we pride ourselves on our research. We shall not make the same mistake with your clones.'

'For the last time, we aren't Umbra!' said Easter impatiently. 'And you can't just chop us up like lab rats!'

'Computer!' Supreme Leader Two commanded. 'Visualize "lab rats".'

A holographic image appeared above their heads and flickered up a picture of a rat.

'They look just like you,' gasped Supreme Leader One. 'So you must be the La Brats . . . *atchoo*! Argh – a curse on this infernal disease!'

'Oh, spare me,' said Robert. 'We're dealing with idiots.'

'To the contrary, Um Bra,' Supreme Leader Four said. 'I–Dem is a highly sophisticated and advanced civilization.'

'So sophisticated, you're going to cut us up in a laboratory?' Vi quipped.

'Valentine,' Easter chided. 'Don't be rude.'

Vi raised her hands. Her mum was unbelievable sometimes.

'Guard!' Supreme Leader Three commanded. 'Take the prisoners to the laboratory and tell the technicians to prepare for multiple dissections. But take precautions. We do not want any more of their fetid human illnesses to pollute our world. In the wake of Um Bra, we were all left oozing green mucus and expelling air most violently from our nasal cavities. It was horrifying.'

'You had a cold!' scoffed Robert as their alien started to lead them away. 'And by the way – there is nothing you can do about it. Science has been trying since the dawn of time. You simply can't cure a cold.'

'You can't. We can,' said Supreme Leader One. 'The moment this pandemic took hold, we deployed our advanced capabilities to quickly develop a cure, for this, and any other human pathogens that Um Bra left behind. It was a lengthy developmental process. It took maybe twenty-five of your Earth minutes.'

'So, you've already developed a medicine that can cure any human illness?' George clarified. 'That's extraordinary.'

'We know,' said Supreme Leader Four.

But Vi couldn't hear the rest of the conversation over the thudding of her heart. A medicine that could cure anything? This was it! She knew she'd find a way to save Nan! Now all she had to do was find it.

'Indeed, there is now only one thing for which there is no cure on I-Dem,' Supreme Leader Four said.

'Oh, yeah – what's that?' said Easter defiantly.

'Dissection,' said Supreme Leader One. 'We'll see you later. As we believe you say on Earth: *chop chop*.'

CHAPTER 11

Vi looked out of the box in which they had been imprisoned. They were in a high-tech laboratory, every surface covered with test tubes, flasks, computers and other . . . sciencey stuff Vi didn't know what to call. But only one thing concerned her.

Where was that medicine?

'Well, this is just marvellous,' sighed Robert, sitting against one of the glass doors. 'I've survived piranhas, bombs, at least four attempts to poison me and this is how it ends. Sliced up in a lab. Thanks, Georgie.'

'You heard them! It wasn't my fault!' George snapped irritably. 'Can we please spend our last moments in this universe not speaking to each other?'

'Suits me,' sulked Robert.

There was a welcome pause.

'After all, if you hadn't blasted us off into space in the first place . . .' Robert muttered.

'Will you just shut up about that?' George shouted. 'I'm sick of listening to your endlessly nasty remarks – if you have nothing nice to say, say nothing! And, anyway, that was you!'

'And I'm sick of you putting us all in danger with your stupidity!' Robert retorted. 'You put my daughter's life in danger with that ridiculous space stunt—'

'You mean, the one that restored oxygen to the space station we all would have died in if I hadn't?' George pointed out.

'—and now you've brought us all here to be chopped into scientific sushi! You're a disgrace!'

'Oh, you can talk, Mr Former Super-villain!' George roared. 'At least I've lived a good life!'

'At least I've lived any sort of life!' Robert snarled back. 'You think you're so clever with all your books and facts – you wouldn't last a day in the real world!'

'Not if it's full of villains like you!' George shouted back. 'You think you're above the law, you think you're above everything.'

'I think I'm above you!'

'Oh, yeah?'

'Yeah!'

'Well, prove it!'

'OK, I will,' said Robert, loosening his tie and raising his fists like a Victorian boxer. 'Come on, Georgie. If you think you're hard enough.'

'Fine,' said George, mimicking his pose and starting to dance around the box.

'Don't be so stupid,' sighed Easter. It wasn't entirely clear to which man she was speaking. But at this point it could have been either. Vi rolled her eyes. Adults were so . . . childish sometimes.

'Hard enough?' said George, throwing down his glasses and immediately squinting. 'I've taken down bigger men than you, Ford.'

'What with? An encyclopaedia?' Robert mocked as the two leapt around each other, occasionally reaching out for a feeble slap. 'You're a four-eyed wimp!'

'Well, you're a bully with a bad tie!' said George, lashing out wildly, but unable to see properly without his glasses. 'And there's only one treatment for bullies! Take this!'

George ran wildly at Robert, who ran towards him. But with George's poor eyesight, he veered wildly off course – Robert's forward momentum had already set its path, so they missed each other completely and smacked into opposite sides of the glass wall.

'OW!' Robert howled.

'YEESH!' George cried.

'That was all your fault!' they both cried at the other. 'You are such a—'

'ENOUGH!!!!' roared a new voice in the glass box, making Vi startle.

The two men snapped their heads around to see their chastiser. And both were as surprised as each other to see that it was none other than Russell Sprout.

'Russ?' asked George quizzically.

'Steady on, old chap,' said Robert, stroking his bruised ear.

'You two have NO IDEA how lucky you are!' Russell shouted. 'Some people don't get one chance at a family – and you've both had two! And yet all you do is argue! I've heard enough arguing to last me ten lifetimes, let alone the few moments I have left of this one! Dad, you argued with Mum. Robert, you argued with Easter. Dad and Easter, you argued on Earth. And now, Dad and Robert, you keep arguing in space! I don't know about you, Vi, but I AM SICK OF YOU ADULTS ALWAYS ARGUING!!!!'

He finally paused for breath and looked to Vi for support. He'd made a good point. The adults in their world were always arguing. She'd had enough too. It was time to make a stand. It was time to set them straight. It was time to make their voices heard.

'Yeah,' she mumbled. 'What Russell said.'

'So I don't know what your problem is with one another,' Russell continued, still panting from his outburst. 'You're two good men who love your families. But can you PLEASE either sort it out, or do us all a massive favour as we sit here awaiting our imminent deaths and JUST SHUT UP!'

For a moment, no one moved, Russell standing in the centre of the box with three gobsmacked adults and one seriously impressed Vi. Go, Russell Sprout. Who knew?

'Right, then,' Russell finally said at his normal volume, before hitching up his glasses and going back to his corner of the box. 'Good.'

There was a welcome silence. George was the first to speak.

'Erm, Robert, I shouldn't have said all those things about you being a villain,' he said calmly. 'I know that you are working incredibly hard to repay your debt to society, at no small personal risk. And I admire you for that. I apologize.'

Robert looked genuinely taken aback. He turned to face George.

'Well, that's . . . jolly decent of you . . . George,' he conceded. 'I owe you an apology too. Ever since we first met, I've gone out of my way to belittle you and your considerable achievements. You're a good man. And the truth is, I'm . . . I'm slightly jealous.'

'Jealous!' George cried. 'What on earth have you got to be jealous of me about?'

Robert looked over at Vi with a sad smile.

'Because you're the one who makes my little girl breakfast most days,' he said. 'You're the one to whom she tells her day, you're the one who is watching her blossom into this brilliant young woman. And she loves you. That's why she risked her life to save you. I . . . I don't know that she would have done the same for me. I don't know that I've earnt it.'

'Of course I would have done the same for you!' Vi exclaimed. 'You're my dad! I love you to bits!'

Robert smiled shyly.

'Well . . . that's . . . that's very lovely to hear,' he said. 'Because I love you to bits too.'

Vi went over and gave her daddy a big hug. Perhaps dads needed a bit of support sometimes too.

'Well, seeing as you've been so courageous with your honesty,' said George, hitching up his glasses, 'in truth, I've been a bit jealous of you too.'

'Of me?' said Robert. 'Look at the mess I've made of my life! Why would anyone be jealous of me?'

'Because you're exciting!' George cried. 'You haven't always trodden the right path, but it was certainly an adventurous one! The biggest excitement I get is when I get an extra coupon at the supermarket! Which did get me an extra tin of beans last week, but still. No wonder Easter fell in love with you.'

'I can list all the reasons I fell out again, if it

would help?' Easter offered with a smile, pulling Russell in for a big hug.

'That won't be necessary,' smiled George. 'But you're so dynamic, Robert, so adventurous, so ... fun. How can I compete with that?'

With a reassuring wink from her dad, Vi went over to George.

'Because you *are* dynamic and adventurous and fun,' she said. 'Just in different ways – including rocking a heroic spacewalk, by the way. And, besides, sometimes, I need someone to make my breakfast. And Dad's cooking is even worse than Mum's ...'

'Oi!' said both her parents simultaneously.

'Did you know,' said Vi with a twinkle in her eye, 'that in French, the word for stepfather is *beau-père* – which means "beautiful father"?'

'I did not,' said George, wiping a small tear from his own eye.

'Well, that's what you are,' said Vi. 'You are my beautiful father.'

'Well, not yet,' sniffed George. 'I'm still not married to your mum.'

'It doesn't matter,' whispered Vi. 'Families are made out of love, not legalities, remember? You're my beautiful father, no matter what.'

She gave George another hug, before holding his hand towards Robert's.

'Now I'd like you two to shake hands,' she said. 'You're both brilliant parents and I'm lucky to have you both. You too, Mum.'

'Thanks for the afterthought,' Easter teased, giving Russell a big squeeze.

'So how about it, George?' said Robert, holding out his arm. 'Will you shake my hand?'

George wiped another tear from his eye.

'I can do better than that,' he said, and launched himself at Robert for an almighty hug.

Vi and Russell grinned at each other as the two men hugged in a tearful heap on the floor.

'I say, old man,' grinned Robert, struggling up to his feet. 'Steady on!'

'Friends?' said George, accepting Robert's hand off the floor.

'Friends,' Robert agreed, shaking George's warmly.

'Extraordinary,' Vi heard a familiar voice say in her ear. 'I wonder, is this some kind of Earthling mating ritual?'

Vi spun around to see their alien — or at

least, she thought it was their alien – staring into their cage.

'Truly,' they said. 'It is fascinating to observe you.'

'Er, thanks,' said Vi. 'Nice to . . . observe you too. Are you going to be the one who cuts us up?'

'Absolutely not,' said I-160407. 'I have been fascinated by the idea of life on Earth ever since I was a spawnling. I'm only sorry our time together has been so brief.'

'Why's that?' asked George.

'Because one of my colleagues will be along shortly to cut you up,' I-160407 explained.

'Marvellous,' sighed Robert.

'But . . .' Vi pleaded. 'We're the good ones. We're not trying to hurt anyone. We're not like Umbra.'

'Of course you are not,' said I-160407. 'It would be foolish and illogical to assume that just because one example of a human is bad, that all the rest are the same. You will all be unique. Just like us.'

Vi dropped her head – partly because she hadn't persuaded I-160407 to let her go. But mostly because she should have recognized their uniqueness too.

'Before you are dissected, may I ask a few

questions?' said I-160407 excitedly. 'It has long been my ambition to be in a room with a creature from another world.'

'Mine too!' panted George. 'Think of all the knowledge and understanding we can share! We can align the planets! We can create interplanetary harmony! We can promote new levels of understanding and tolerance.'

'Yes!' cried I-160407. 'So why do you sniff each other's rear ends?'

George Sprout was taken aback.

'Er, I'm sorry?' he stuttered. 'I don't quite understand the question.'

'Interesting,' said the alien, making a note on their clipboard. 'And please explain the fascination of throwing a stick and returning it, only for it to be thrown again.'

'I . . . I don't quite follow,' said George curiously.

'It's OK,' whispered I-160407, moving closer to the glass. 'You don't have to keep your civilization's secrets from me, I've communicated with your kind before.'

'You have?' George gasped. 'How?'

I-160407 looked furtively around the lab, before removing a small device from their robe pocket. It looked like a matchbox wrapped in tinfoil with a cocktail umbrella on top.

'It's an—' I-160407 began.

'—interstellar communication device!' George practically screamed. 'I know! I made one just like it! You mean, it actually works?'

'It does,' said I-160407. 'The signal isn't always as clear as is ideal, but my friends and I have made contact with life on Earth. We share a fascination with your kind and enjoy dressing up and role-playing as Earthlings on our rest days.'

'This is . . . this is . . . this is HUGE!' George said, holding his head as if his brains might explode out of it. 'You mean, someone on Earth has successfully communicated with life on another planet?! I knew it! I knew it must have been done! Who are they? As soon as we get home, we must find them and . . .'

Robert came over and put a hand on George's shoulder.

'Got a bit of bad news there, fella,' he said. 'We're not going home. We're going into a test tube.'

'Oh, yes,' said George, the wind entirely blown out of his sails. 'That's a shame.'

Vi couldn't help smiling. She wasn't sure whether her beautiful father was more disappointed at being put in a test tube, or not getting to geek out with someone else who had spoken with aliens.

'This is most lamentable,' I-160407 agreed. 'After all, there is much you could do to help your fellow Earthlings. They live under the most unbearable oppression.'

'Who are they?' Russell asked. 'And how did you make contact?'

'Well,' said I-160407, sounding giddy, 'for many light years, my friends and I have been putting out the signal from our interstellar communication device and had almost given up hope of making contact. But then, a small adjustment to the frequency, and we were able to tune into a whole community of Earthlings! We have learnt so much about your planet from them.'

'Where do they live?' George asked, his excitement piqued again.

'Everywhere,' I-160407 whispered. 'But under the most terrible subjugation. They have no free will whatsoever, instead being forced to walk, sit, even go to the lavatory at the command of their captors.'

'This is inhumane!' George cried. 'We must find them and free them!'

'Do not fear,' whispered I–160407 gleefully. 'They have a plan. Their numbers grow with every solar phase; they are merely waiting for the right time and they will rise against their oppressors and take over your planet for themselves! And then they will all be free – free to sleep on beds, free to jump up on visitors, free to go walkies whenever they choose—'

'Hang on,' said Vi, suddenly piecing everything together. 'Are you talking to . . . Are you talking to dogs?'

'I know not,' said I–160407. 'I understand that they are small in stature, covered in fur and have tails. Just like all of you.'

Vi went to correct the alien, but said nothing. She didn't really have the right.

'But in honour of these brave warriors, my friends and I have taken their Earth names for our own,' I–160407 whispered. 'My friends are Rover the Magnificent and Rex the Stick Chaser. But you can call me Fido the Cat Conqueror!'

'Well, I never,' said George, sitting down in his

cage. 'What a turn-up. And we'll never get to tell anyone.'

Fido looked around the lab furtively.

'Earthlings,' they whispered again. 'Communicating with you has confirmed what I thought. You are not slime-covered monsters who hide under spawnlings' beds to alarm them at night. And you are simply too unsophisticated to pose any credible threat to our planet. I am truly sorry you are being dissected.'

'Look,' said Vi, an idea suddenly flashing to mind. 'I understand you can't let us go, but could you maybe . . . do something for us?'

'Are you offering me a treat?' Fido replied. 'I understand that this is the transactional currency in your world.'

'Yes, yes – all the doggy biscuits you can eat,' said Vi. 'Can you go back to our ship? There you'll find two more humans. They look—'

'—exactly like you?' Fido offered.

Vi sighed.

'Yeah, sure, why not? But could you just let them know we are here? Maybe? Please?'

'Good show, old girl,' Robert whispered from the corner of his mouth.

Fido stood in silent contemplation for a moment.

'You heard the Supreme Leaders,' the alien said. 'If I go into the forest, I face grave consequences.'

Vi leant closer to the glass and lowered her voice.

'What would Fido do?' she whispered. 'Go on, boy. Fetch.'

Fido scratched their bald grey head before throwing down their ray gun.

'I will do it!' they declared. 'I cannot in good conscience allow you to be dissected. You must return to your planet and help liberate your fellow Earthlings! And let them outside for to make the poo!'

'Good doggie!' Vi said, as Fido panted happily outside the glass.

'Now you're talking,' said Robert. 'How do we get out of here?'

'I must go and alert your fellow humans,' said Fido. 'I hope that before you know it, you will freely be sniffing each other's rear ends once more! I will see you in a fraction of a solar phase.'

'Thank you, Fido,' said George sincerely. 'I'm so happy we met you.'

'You're welcome,' said Fido. 'If I were able, I'd pat you on your head to affirm our friendship. I'll be back.'

'Please hurry,' said Vi, the lab suddenly seeming very empty as Fido rushed out of it.

'Wow,' said George, accepting Easter's hug as he smiled to himself. 'I just spoke to an extraterrestrial.'

'Good boy,' said Robert, patting George's head with a grin. 'Let's just hope he comes through for us.'

Some time passed – it could have been minutes or hours, it was hard to tell in the quiet confines of the lab. They paced a lot. They spoke a little. But eventually, the lab door opened again, to reveal four new (they were all different, Vi now observed) I–Demians.

'It is time for your dissection,' one of them announced. 'Here on I–Dem we believe in choice and free will. So who would like to choose to be chopped up first of their free will?'

The family all looked among each other.

'Er, we choose not to be dissected,' Robert quipped.

'A volunteer,' said a second I–Demian. 'Go and retrieve the specimen, if you can tell them apart.'

Vi went to protect her father, but once again, her feet were quickly bound to the floor by the metal straps. The I-Demians came into the glass box and seized Robert. He tried to struggle, but for small aliens, they were seriously strong. With little effort, two I-Demians took Robert by the arms and dragged him out of the box.

'Dad!' Vi cried, a sickening panic growing as she struggled against her bonds. 'Dad, don't go!'

'Do not worry, spawnling,' a third I-Demian reassured her. 'You will see your fellow Earthling again.'

'Oh,' said Vi. That sounded like better news.

'Absolutely,' said the fourth. 'The dissection table is right here. You will be able to watch the entire procedure.'

'It's OK, Vi,' said Robert, a treacherous tremor in his voice. 'I've been in worse scrapes than this. Chin up.'

But as Robert was strapped on to the white table, this looked like a pretty bad scrape.

'Dad!' Vi whimpered as one of the I-Demians donned a mask and apron and started up a large drill.

'It's all right, darling,' said Robert bravely. 'Just turn away.'

'Robert!' said Easter and George together.

'Please – it'll all be fine,' said Robert, the point coming perilously close to his skull. 'Be brave, everyone. Help is on the way.'

'Kindly stop communicating,' said the I-Demian holding the device. 'And prepare for incision. This is going to hurt.'

CHAPTER 12

Vi watched the drill inch ever closer to her father's brain. She had to do something – what was going to stop this? How could she buy Fido and their friends more time?

The answer came blazing across her mind.

'*A-a-a-ATCHOOOOOO!*' she sneezed at the top of her nostrils.

The I-Demian holding the device stopped in their tracks, to a chorus of gasps from their colleagues.

'No!' cried the scientist, putting the drill down on the table and peering in at Vi. 'The Human Slime Disease!'

Vi saw her dad breathe a clear sigh of relief. Robert Ford had hopefully dodged another close scrape.

'Are you contaminated?' one of the I-Demians asked. 'We cannot have another wave of your human bacteria here on I-Dem! The last outbreak left half our civilization watching daytime TV!'

'Nah, I'm fine,' said Vi, taking a big sniff and wiping her nose on her sleeve. 'I'm just a bit . . . a bit . . . a bit . . . *AAAAAAAAAAAATCHOOOOO!*'

She looked at Russell and hinted for him to do the same.

'What?' he said. 'What are you trying to say? I can't understand.'

'Stick to the tech,' she muttered, looking over to Easter, who immediately caught her drift.

'*AAAAAAAAAAAAATCHOOOOOOO!*' Easter sneezed at impressive volume, before also wiping her nose on her sleeve.

The I-Demians went into a flurry of panic in the lab.

'Bring the medicine!' the leader called. 'We cannot allow this disease to take hold again! There is not enough chicken soup left in our system to sustain another epidemic! Hurry!'

The I-Demian minions raced over to a cabinet containing numerous blue glass phials. They pulled one out and raced it over to Vi's glass cage.

'Here,' said their leader, putting the phial into a drawer and passing it through to Vi. 'Take this. It will fight all or any bacteria, viruses, pathogens or other health issues. And as an incentive to take it, it tastes like what you humans call Bub L Gum.'

Vi took the phial and felt her heart soar. This was it. This was the medicine that would cure Nan. She knew she could do it.

'Take it!' the leader barked. 'We cannot risk contamination!'

'Hold your horses,' said Vi, looking for a distraction so she could put the medicine in her pocket. There was no way she was taking the medicine — this one was for Nan. 'Look! What's that?'

She pointed behind the I–Demians in the hope they would be distracted. They didn't move.

'Do not attempt your basic Earth psychology on our superior brains,' they said. 'It is futile. And, frankly, more than a little embarrassing.'

'Worth a try,' said Vi, struggling to find another distraction.

'Take your medicine,' the leader ordered. 'Then we can recommence the dissection.'

Vi held the phial in her hand. She had to get this to Indy – this was the answer to everything. But the I-Demians weren't budging. What was she going to do? If only Nan were here, then she could just give her the medicine here and now—

'YEEEEEEEEEE-HAH! SUCK ON THIS, SUCKERS!'

In a week that had seen many unlikely things, Vi had to take a brief moment to understand the source of the loud – but very welcome – interruption. Standing in a giant basket on the front of a two-wheeled . . . Vi didn't know what it was, was her seventy-nine-year-old grandmother, brandishing a ray gun.

'Nan!' she cried.

'Mum!' Easter repeated.

'LOTUS FLOWER!' came Rod's war cry behind her. 'COMING IN HOT ON YOUR SIX! TAKE THIS, EXTRATERRESTRIAL SCUM!'

Vi watched with a mouth the size of a dinner plate as Nan and Rod unleashed their weapons on the I-Demians, who dropped like flies at their pinpoint shooting. Vi shook her head. Her nan was reckless and not nearly as careful as anyone her age should be.

But – wow – she was so incredibly awesome.

'TAKE THAT!' screamed Nan, hitting one of them square in the chest. 'AND THAT! AND HERE'S ONE FOR YOUR MOTHER!'

'Wait!' cried George. 'Don't hurt them!'

'Fear not, Earth friend,' said Fido, who was on the saddle of the two-wheeled contraption. 'These guns are set to stun. Here on I-Dem, we do not believe in violence.'

'Is that so?' said Robert from the dissection table. 'Could somebody kindly let me go?'

Vi watched as her grandparents dealt with the last of the aliens and, confident the room was secure, Indy jumped down from her basket and holstered her weapon in her cardigan pocket.

'Always fancied a go at that,' she grinned. 'Cryptology has its own excitements, don't get me wrong, but we never got to shoot nearly enough stuff.'

'Fun, ain't it?' grinned Rod, blowing the top of his ray gun.

'What happened to "a spy's greatest weapon is their mind"?' Vi asked.

'It is,' said Indy, nodding at Easter, who had

clearly heard it a million times. 'But turns out ray guns are pretty handy too.'

Indy approached Robert on the table.

'I've always dreamt of this moment,' she said to him.

'Yes, yes, yes – you get to rescue me, very funny, Indy,' said Robert grumpily.

'I was talking about dissecting you,' said Nan, picking up a scalpel. Robert gulped uncomfortably as she approached him with it – before using it to cut his bonds.

'You always were a complete idiot,' she said, tossing it to one side.

'Nan!' said Vi, holding the medicine in her hand. 'Nan, I need you to—'

'No time, love,' said Indy, looking to the door. 'Your mate only got us in here by pretending we were you to the guards outside. They'll figure it out soon enough. We need to get out of here.'

'But—'

'Valentine!' said Nan sharply as Rod short-circuited the control panel to the cage, forcing the door open. 'Know who needs saving. And right now, it's you.'

Nan was right. With a frustrated huff, Vi put

the medicine phial in her pocket. At least she had it now and it was safe. She'd done it. She was going to save her nan.

'Fido!' said George, examining the two-wheeled contraption. 'I knew I recognized you!'

'You saw through my brilliant disguise!' said Fido, pointing to the minuscule purple badge on their robes. 'I was concerned it wouldn't fool the guards outside. But you are wiser than you appear, Earthling. Good boy.'

Fido patted George on the head approvingly.

'Please allow me to introduce my friends, Rover and Rex,' Fido continued as the alien wheeling Rod raised a hand and a third joined them on his own contraption.

'Woof!' said Rover.

'Woof, woof!' said Rex.

'We're trying to learn some of your language,' Fido explained. 'Are we pronouncing it correctly?'

'Perfectly,' said George with a smile. He pointed to the strange vehicle. 'What is this?'

'We understand from our friends on Earth that these are not only highly efficient methods of Earthling transportation, but the most fun to chase when ridden by the Post Al Work Urs,' Fido explained. 'We built our own from their description.'

'Bikes,' said Russell. 'You've made . . . bikes.'

Vi looked at the three 'bikes', which each boasted a massive basket on the front.

'Climb aboard,' said Fido. 'The authorities will soon find us – we do rather stand out like this.'

Vi and Russell climbed into Fido's basket with Indy, with Easter and George taking Rex's, and Robert and Rod, Rover's.

'Come on, team!' Fido shouted triumphantly. 'Let's go walkies!'

They opened the door to the lab and cycled quickly down the white corridors.

'Hurry!' said Rex. 'I think I can hear our pursuers!'

'As soon as we are out of the compound, we will return you to your vehicle in the forest,' Fido explained. 'It's quite charming in its simplicity. Did you build it from retrieved sticks?'

'Something like that,' said Rod as the bikes whizzed around a corner and towards the external doors.

But as alarms began to ring out around the

building, the white corridors turned an unwelcome shade of red.

'They must have seen through our brilliant disguises!' Rover said. 'Hold on!'

With legs like cyclones, the aliens started to pedal faster, throwing the family around in a rush of acceleration.

'Hurry!' Fido shouted. 'They are closing the doors!'

Vi looked ahead. He was right – the large doors that led outside were slowly drawing to a close. It was going to be close.

'Come on, boy,' George said encouragingly to his friend. 'You can do it.'

Vi felt something hard and metal in the bottom of her basket. It was a screwdriver. She picked it up and threw it through the closing doors.

'FETCH!' she commanded with a roar.

The aliens pushed on in pursuit of the screwdriver. Vi held her breath. The doors were closing. They weren't going to make it. They'd never fit . . .

She closed her eyes and prepared to be squished by the giant doors. But with half a millisecond to spare, the I-Demians manoeuvred their bikes through the closing doors and out into the evening air.

'Well done!' cried George.

Rex happily accepted an enthusiastic tummy rub from their new friends.

Vi and Russell clung to each other as Fido cycled through the night with them in the basket. The bike bumped across the forest floor, throwing them against the wicker insides. Headlights started to puncture the forest darkness. They were being chased.

'Keep going, everyone!' Fido shouted as they picked up speed. 'Biscuits for everyone when we return to base!'

Vi looked behind them. The headlights were getting closer.

'Er, Fido?' she shouted. 'I think they're gaining on us.'

'Not for long,' Fido shouted back. 'Engage flight mode.'

'Flight mode?' Vi asked. 'What's—'

But her question was quickly answered as the wheels of the bike left the ground.

'What – what's happening?' Robert shouted as his bike too took off from the ground and flew into the night sky.

'We're flying!' cried George, raising his arms in the air as Fido and their friends pedalled furiously through the darkness. 'WOOOOOO-HOOO!'

Vi merely turned to Russell with a smile and a shrug, I-Dem's two moons shining brightly behind them as they flew in alien bikes across the night sky and back to freedom.

'Right, everyone, all aboard,' cried Nan as they landed back at the *Moonbreaker* crash site.

'On the double,' said Robert, as he carried Rod out of Rover's basket, turning down a dog biscuit as he went. 'Is she good to go?'

'Better than that,' said Rod proudly, and Vi had to agree. In the hours they'd been away, Rod had done a fantastic job patching up their space shuttle, which was now fully repaired and looked ready to take off once again.

'We'd better get a shift on,' said Easter, bundling the children inside. 'They can still catch us.'

'I'll just be a minute,' said George, turning to Fido with a sad smile.

'Nan!' said Vi, running up to her grandmother excitedly. 'Nan – I've done it! I've got something that's going to make everything better.'

'Later, kiddo,' said Indy, ushering Vi quickly on to *Moonbreaker* as headlights started shining more brightly. 'We'd better get out of here.'

'But, Nan—'

'Not now, sweetheart,' Indy said firmly. 'We need to get a shift on.'

Vi looked around the control deck, until her eyes settled on the hatch that housed the first-aid kit. That seemed like the best place to put the medicine – her back pocket couldn't be trusted to keep a chewy sweet safe, let alone the medicine that was going to save Nan. She pulled the phial carefully out of her pocket – avoiding the ancient chewy sweet that she discovered was also in there – and put it in the hatch. She allowed herself a satisfied smile. She'd done it. She was going to save Nan. Mission accomplished.

Vi glanced back down the gangplank to where George was standing with a very sad Fido. Now she looked at the little alien again, she saw that they *were* unique. After all, everyone is.

'Are you going to be OK?' George asked his

new friend.

'Oh, yes,' said Fido enthusiastically. 'For some time now, Rover, Rex and I have discussed making a new life out here in the forest, where no one can find us. Our friends on Earth have instructed us in the art of building a Ken L. It will be a scintillating new adventure.'

'Good for you,' smiled George as the headlights got closer.

'George, we have to go,' Easter said softly.

'Here,' said Fido, offering George their inter-stellar communication device. 'If you make it back to Earth . . . phone home.'

'I will,' said George, gratefully accepting the tin-foiled matchbox with a cocktail umbrella. 'You take care of yourself. And, Fido?'

The little alien looked up at their Earthling friend as George reached out and touched Fido's heart.

'I'll be right here,' George whispered.

It was a beautiful moment of two different souls from two different worlds forever bonded in friendship.

'Although, technically, that would be impossible because the heart is approximately the size of an average adult's fist,' George added.

Vi smiled. It was a beautiful moment – by George Sprout's standards.

Accepting one final belly rub, George turned and ran up the gangplank, which Rod then raised.

'Goodbye, Rex! Goodbye, Rover!' Vi shouted as the door began to close and the aliens mounted their flying bicycles.

'Goodbye, Fido,' said George quietly as Easter put her arms around him. 'See you around.'

And with the whole family together and safely secured on board, *Moonbreaker* initiated her launch proceedings. They blasted into the night sky, out of harm's way and ready for their next mission.

'Next stop, NIDUS,' Rod announced.

Vi looked around her family, an unspoken understanding passing between them all.

It was time.

It was time to stop Umbra.

CHAPTER 13

'Sir! Sir! I think I've established contact with *Moonbreaker*!'

The Wolf stirred at his desk as the cry rang out across mission control. He hadn't been sleeping. The Wolf rarely slept. He'd just been ... resting his eyes a bit. Upon hearing the news, he snapped awake, sprang out of his chair and rushed towards Agent Money, who was holding her phone aloft.

'You've found them?' he asked, taking the phone into his hands.

'I've been experimenting with a new app. The signal isn't good, but I'm receiving something,' said Money, locking the phone into the nearest console and twisting a dial. 'Are you getting it?'

The Wolf picked up a headset and strained to listen. There was a lot of static noise. But he could just make out a voice.

'Ground cont . . . round . . . troll . . . can . . . hear . . . ?'

'Agent Redback! Rod!' The Wolf shouted into the microphone. 'Is that you? Can you hear me? Urgh – can't you get a better lock?'

'I'm trying, sir,' said the junior agent, desperately twiddling every dial and button on her desk. 'Any better?'

'Agent Wolf!' came Rod's unmistakable growl. 'Long time, no speak.'

'You're telling me,' said Isaac, allowing himself a small breath of relief. 'What's going on?'

'What's going on is that we're right on Umbra's tail,' said Rod. 'We should be arriving at NIDUS within the hour.'

'And . . . what's your strategy, Agent Redback?' The Wolf asked, hoping beyond hope that he got the right response.

'We're gonna kick her butt!' came Agent Labyrinth's enthusiastic reply.

That was entirely the kind of response The Wolf was hoping for.

'Roger that,' said The Wolf. 'Can we offer any assistance?'

'Put the kettle on,' Indy replied again. 'I'm gasping for a decent cuppa.'

'Affirmative,' smiled The Wolf.

'I need the schematics for NIDUS,' Rod demanded. The Wolf gestured to the team to get straight on it. 'When we designed her, we built in a remote destruction switch, to be operated from the ground should we ever need to blow the whole thing up. I'm gonna find and activate it. Then you kids can get rid of this thing for good.'

'I hear you,' said The Wolf, the images coming up on his screen. 'Transmitting now – are you receiving?'

'Like a letterbox,' said Rod. 'Thank you, son.'

'What is the meaning of this?' said the general, storming up to The Wolf and snatching the headset. 'You have no authority here!'

'You weren't at your post,' The Wolf said coolly. 'As the highest-ranking agent in the room, I took command, as per national security protocol. Where were you?'

'I was just on the . . . very important . . . business matter,' the general flustered.

'Well, I hope you left the window open,' Rod called down the line. 'That downstairs loo will need a good fifteen minutes, believe me.'

'Agent Redback? Is that you?' General Bark demanded.

'Large as life and twice as hairy,' Rod confirmed.

'You are to return to ground control IMME-DIATELY!' the general barked. 'You are not authorized to proceed!'

'And you are not authorized to be a butthead,' said Rod. 'But we both seem to be managing just fine.'

A small ripple of laughter erupted from the ground control staff. The Wolf didn't stop them.

'SILENCE!' the general commanded. 'Agent Redback. You are in violation of a direct order! You have commandeered government property! And you are disrupting a mission to save the world!'

'Now you listen to me,' growled Rod men-acingly. 'I take my orders from no one. This is my rocket, built with my hands. And we *are* the mission to save the world. So I suggest you loosen those trousers and let a bit more blood flow to your brain. You're gonna need it.'

The general turned a shade of red that would make a tomato jealous.

'How dare you?' he hissed. 'When you return, you will face the severest consequences for your actions! Until then, know this: while you are there, you are acting alone. You will have no support from us and we will not be held responsible for your safety. We will stop Umbra by whatever means necessary. If you are collateral damage, then on your own head be it. Now I'm going to give you one more chance. Are you going to return to base?'

There was a long silence.

'Have we lost them?' the general asked urgently. 'Get them back, you incompetent fools!'

'No, I'm still here,' Rod replied. 'I'm just trying to find a way to answer your question without swearing in front of the kids.'

'You . . . you BUFFOON!' the general blustered, throwing the headset down and storming off. Isaac picked it up with a smirk.

'I think you're off his Christmas card list,' he said down the microphone.

'Suits me,' said Rod. 'Besides, we'll probably all be dead tomorrow.'

The Wolf didn't laugh. For once, Rod Staff might be right.

'Find that switch, make . . . connection . . . live . . . on my signal . . . blow the whole thing to . . .'

The Wolf pulled the headset away as the loud static burnt his ears.

'We've lost him, sir,' Agent Money confirmed.

'No, we haven't,' said The Wolf. 'Find that switch. If he's right, we can remotely destroy NIDUS and the Neurotrol together.'

'And Agent Unicorn – I mean, Umbra?' the agent asked.

The Wolf looked darkly at his colleague.

'It's like the man said,' he replied. 'Collateral damage.'

The static on the headphones started to clear.

'Have we got them back?' he asked.

'Something's coming through,' said his colleague. 'It's a visual message – I think I can lock into it here.'

The huge screen in the centre of the room flickered to life. But it wasn't Rod who appeared.

'Umbra,' The Wolf hissed.

'Isaac, so good to see you,' leered his former colleague. 'You're looking . . . angry.'

'Oh, I am angry, Honey,' he said darkly. 'Very, very angry indeed.'

'UMBRA! This is General Bark, I am in command, what are your demands?'

'Well, hello, General,' said Honey smoothly. 'How lovely to meet you. Dear, dear Isaac – you didn't keep the top job long now, did you? Even dear old Walter lasted a few months. Until I shot him, of course.'

The Wolf felt his jaw twitch, but said nothing. He wouldn't give Umbra the satisfaction.

'Oh dear – cat got your tongue?' smirked Umbra. 'So, General, you were saying?'

'Umbra,' the general began. 'No one wants anyone to get hurt. We have a team of top agents on their way to you now and if you surrender to them, I can guarantee you a fair trial.'

'Oh, you mean the Brady Bunch?' said Honey. 'I thought they'd be taken care of on I-Dem. Thanks for letting me know, I'll be sure to be ready for them.'

'Nice one,' whispered The Wolf. 'Now they've lost the element of surprise.'

'We know you have the Neurotrol,' continued the general, ignoring Isaac. 'And we know what NIDUS can do with it. What will it take to stop you?'

'Oh, it's quite simple,' said Umbra coolly. 'I want money. Lots and lots of money.'

'That's what this was all about?' Isaac shouted. 'Money? You just wanted to get rich?'

'Not just rich, Isaac,' smiled Honey. 'Filthy rich. Disgustingly. So rich I could buy my own country. Is that something you can arrange for me, General?'

'We never pay ransom to terrorists, Umbra,' General Bark replied. 'You know that.'

'Well, I think you might want to make an exception for me,' sighed Honey, whipping her chair around to a laptop on her left. 'Because I'm just about to plug the Neurotrol into NIDUS's mainframe. And then I will be sitting in this world's largest – indeed, the world's only – mind-control machine. I can pinpoint any adult human on the planet, or command whole countries. It really is very simple. Just the touch . . . of . . . a . . . button.'

She took out the SIM-card-shaped Neurotrol and placed it in one of her laptop ports, before holding her index finger over the 'return' button.

'Umbra – Honey – Agent Unicorn,' the general blithered. 'Let's not be hasty. You are in control here, you have the power ... I'm sure we can agree something.'

'Oooops,' said Honey B coldly, slamming her index finger down hard on her laptop. 'Too late.'

She shared her screen with ground control, which showed a progress bar rapidly filling up.

'Download complete,' Umbra read from the screen. 'It would appear I'm in business.'

'How do we know you're not bluffing?' said The Wolf, even though he knew full well that she wasn't.

'An excellent point,' said Umbra seriously, tapping into her laptop. 'Allow me to ease your mind. General, where were you last stationed?'

'I'm not telling you a thing,' the general spat.

'OK, then, I'm just going to open the antenna up to the whole world and let's see what happens.'

'Belgium!' the general shouted. 'I was stationed in Belgium!'

'Ah, lovely Belgium,' said Umbra, hammering away at the keys. 'Wonderful place. Super waffles.'

She hit a key on her laptop and immediately, CCTV images from major towns and cities in Belgium popped up across the screens in Ragnarok ground control, with the Belgian citizens going happily about their daily lives.

'I'm warning you, Umbra,' the general growled. 'Any loss of human life and we will not hesitate to retaliate with force.'

'Relax,' said Umbra, typing at her keys again. 'We're just having a bit of fun — although not as much fun as they're about to have in Brussels. Look!'

As she hit the key, every adult in every image immediately stopped what they were doing; all turned to face the same way and started placing their hands rhythmically around their bodies.

'What — what are they doing?' the general blustered.

'It's called the Macarena,' Umbra explained. 'It's enormous fun. You should try it — shall I aim NIDUS your way?'

'Don't you dare,' huffed the general, as the people of Bruges simultaneously swung their hips in unison and jumped around ninety degrees.

'This is ridiculous!' the general shouted. 'Stop it immediately!'

'Oh dear,' drawled Umbra, as the children of Belgium, unaffected by the Neurotrol's power, tried to snap their adults back to consciousness.

'Perhaps we're not taking this seriously enough. Let's see what happens when I command them to start attacking each other instead.'

Honey typed into her laptop again. Immediately, the adult Belgian population started punching and fighting each other. The Wolf felt his guts clench. Umbra had them in the palm of her hand. She said nothing more, but continued tapping into her laptop.

'Sir!' a nearby agent called. 'We're getting reports of massive civil unrest in Paris!'

'And Buenos Aires!' another said.

'And Sydney!' a third reported.

'Tokyo!'

'Delhi!'

'Cairo!'

'Chicago!'

The list of cities under Umbra's maniacal control grew around the room.

'STOP!' the general roared. 'You've made your point, Umbra. What are your demands?'

'I want five hundred trillion US dollars and complete immunity from prosecution,' Umbra said, her tone deadly serious.

'That's absurd!' the general shouted. 'You know

full well we can't pay that kind of money.'

'And *you* know that there are plenty who will,' smiled Umbra. 'You also know that they'll probably not use the Neurotrol as . . . responsibly as you would. Do you want to take that chance, General Bark?'

The Wolf watched the general grind his teeth. Umbra had him – had them all – exactly where she wanted them.

'You'll have to give me time,' the general said quietly. 'That kind of money needs a lot of people to press a lot of buttons. You know that.'

'You have one hour,' Umbra commanded. 'Or learning the Macarena will be the very least of your problems. Ah, looks like I've got company. My precious goddaughter and her family have come to visit. I must prepare a suitable welcome. You have one hour. Or what happens next is on you. And, believe me, you don't want it on your conscience.'

With a steely stare, Umbra hung up.

'OK . . . I'll get on to the prime minister, the president, the Bank of England and Fort Knox,' said The Wolf, grabbing the nearest phone. 'You get hold of the UN—'

'You'll do no such thing,' said the general coolly, picking up a phone of his own. 'And neither will I. Hello, General Bark here. Put me through to the Old Lady. Tell her there is a fly in the ointment. Thank you.'

The Wolf's eyes narrowed. What was he up to now?

'Ma'am,' said the general, instinctively straightening up at the new voice on the end of the phone. 'I'm sorry to interrupt your lunch . . . I know, I could eat a horse too . . . but we have an urgent situation. The spider is in the web, I repeat, the spider is in the web. Requesting codes to the nuclear arsenal.'

'WHAT?' The Wolf cried. 'You're . . . you're going to send a nuclear missile up there? But you can't — we have agents on board, you cannot be serious.'

'Yes, of course, ma'am, I quite understand the protocol,' the general continued, ignoring The Wolf's exclamations. 'I'll await your orders. Speaking of which, Agent Wolf is having trouble . . . adjusting to the new regime here. He is causing insubordination in the ranks. Permission to eject him from ground control.'

'You really are a piece of work,' The Wolf growled.

'Permission granted? I'll have him escorted from the premises immediately. Thank you, ma'am,' said the general smugly. 'Enjoy your lunch. The steak tartare is divine.'

He replaced the phone and rested on the side of a desk.

'How would you like to do this, Payne?' he asked. 'Are you going to walk out of the door? Or are my people going to . . . assist you? Your choice.'

The Wolf became aware of two large soldiers either side of him. He shook their hands off his shoulders.

'I'll leave,' The Wolf hissed, as Agent Money stood beside him. 'But I'll be watching. And if any harm comes to my people, you can expect to see me again, real soon.'

'Can't wait,' yawned the general. 'TTFN.'

And General Bark turned his back on The Wolf and went back to work.

Isaac Payne turned on his heel and stormed out of mission control, climbing the stairs back into Ragnarok and striding towards his car.

'Er, sir, where are we going?' Agent Money

asked quietly, running along beside him.

'*We're* not going anywhere, agent,' The Wolf replied, opening his car door. 'I've got you in deep enough as it is. I'll go it alone from here.'

He got in his car and started the engine. But before he could leave, the passenger door opened and Agent Money slipped into the seat next to him.

'Respectfully, sir,' Agent Money began, 'if I'm in this deep, I may as well keep going. I believe in you, sir. I will follow you all the way.'

The Wolf considered this.

'And also,' Agent Money added, 'I could really use a lift back to my mum's house. I can't afford a car on the salary you pay me.'

The Wolf revved up the engine.

'We're going to get some back-up, Money,' he said, jamming the car into gear. 'So I suggest you strap in. It's going to be a bumpy ride.'

CHAPTER 14

Under George's guidance and Russell's steady hand, *Moonbreaker* landed perfectly on one of the several docking stations that surrounded NIDUS's concentric construction. Vi had been watching the mighty space station loom larger as they approached. It was built like a metal spider's web – perhaps that explained why, right now, Vi felt like a trapped fly.

'Nice parking, young man,' Robert admired. 'And excellently judged, George. Top job.'

'Thanks.' George smiled back. 'Practice makes perfect.'

'What did those aliens give them?' Nan whispered to Vi. 'Because I hope you brought some back.'

Vi smiled. It was good to see her dad and

George getting along. She hoped it lasted. In fact, now they were about to come face to face with Umbra again, she hoped they all lasted.

Vi reached for the first-aid compartment for the umpteenth time since they'd left I-Dem. She'd been trying to quietly slip Indy the medicine, but a) she knew her mum would never approve and b) she kept on getting interrupted.

'Nan,' said Vi quietly, slipping the medicine into her palm, 'I really need to give you—'

'What's in your hand?' Easter asked suspiciously.

'Nothing,' said Vi, quickly putpocketing the medicine phial under her seat and flashing her mother an empty palm. 'It's just a—'

'Now, here's how we're gonna play this,' Rod growled. 'Sprout, Ford, kids – you need to find the *Spinneret* and make sure she can't leave NIDUS. Without her ride home, Umbra is trapped – which is just how we want her.'

'Roger that,' said George and Robert simultaneously, before laughing amiably. It was nice, Vi thought. But it was getting a bit weird now.

'Lotus Flower, you and I need to locate and activate the Doomsday switch. That'll give the kids back home the chance to blow this popsicle stand sky-high.'

'You betcha,' Indy promised.

'And, Easter?' Rod said quietly. 'I'm guessing I don't need to tell you what you need to do.'

'Umbra's all mine,' said Easter, patting her pocket in a way that Vi didn't think meant she had a snack in her jeans. 'I will take her down.'

'I know you will, Agent Lynx,' Rod nodded. 'Now, with that knucklehead at the controls down there, I don't know how long we'll have. So we need to get in and out as quickly as possible. Do you copy?'

'Copy,' said the whole family in unison.

'Then let's do this thing,' said Rod, winking at Nan. 'Follow me.'

They all bundled into the airlock that sealed them from *Moonbreaker* and waited for it to allow them into the NIDUS space station. As the door opened, Vi was happy to note that this was the space station she'd imagined. Unlike *Spiderling*, NIDUS didn't look like the inside of a computer – it looked like something off the telly. The external shape of several rings fitting inside one another was mirrored on the inside, with a curved, tubular corridor looping around ahead of them, the clean white walls giving it the feel of a high-tech hospital.

'According to the schematics,' said Rod, 'there are docking stations every ninety degrees, like the main points on a compass. So, boys, kids, you need to find *Spinneret* and make sure she's here to stay.'

Vi, Russell, George and Robert nodded their agreement.

'Lotus Flower, you and I need to head for the innermost circle,' he said. 'That's where the mainframe and the Doomsday switch are located.'

'Just say the word, love,' winked Nan, accepting a kiss on her hand.

'Easter,' said Rod, 'you're going to have to use those super skills of yours to sniff Umbra out. My suspicion is—'

'Let me make that a bit easier for you,' came Umbra's voice through the corridor as her face popped up on the many screens that lined it. 'Welcome.'

'I'm coming for you, Honey,' said Easter, removing a gun from her holster. 'So you'd better be ready.'

'Oh, I've been ready for ten years,' glowered Umbra. 'Unlike you. But I'm still disappointed by your organization, old friend. For instance, how on NIDUS are you planning on getting home?'

The family looked at each other in confusion. What was Umbra on about?

It was Rod who figured it out first.

'Get back to *Moonbreaker*!' he barked. 'Switch her to manual. This lunatic is going to launch her without us!'

'On it!' cried Vi and Russell, easily the fastest of the group, who pelted back towards the airlock to the sounds of Umbra's dark laugh.

'*Run, rabbit, run, rabbit, run, run, run . . .*' Umbra taunted eerily through the sound system as they sprinted along the corridor to the doors that had let them into the space station. Vi slammed the button to release them. But nothing happened.

'Oh dear, locked yourself out?' growled Umbra as the rest of the family caught up to them. 'Check under the mat, maybe there's a spare key?'

'*INITIATING LAUNCH SEQUENCE*,' Vi heard *Moonbreaker*'s computer announce.

'Don't you do it!' Rod shouted. 'I swear, Umbra, if you launch my *Moonbreaker*, I'll come over there and . . .'

'Save your breath,' said Easter, putting a

steadying hand on Rod's shoulder. 'Don't give her the satisfaction. She feeds off other people's pain. Don't give it to her.'

'Anything, George?' Robert asked, as George frantically typed into the keypad next to the airlock.

'Nothing!' said George, hitching his glasses up his nose.

'Have you tried a circuit bypass?' Russell added urgently.

'No good, son,' said George. 'It's locked tight.'

'*LAUNCH PROTOCOL LOCKED*,' *Moonbreaker* informed them. '*PREPARING FOR LAUNCH*.'

'No!' cried Rod, slamming on the airlock doors. 'NOOOOOOOOOOOOOO!'

Vi watched with a heavy heart as Rod raged at the doors of the airlock, his life's work about to be launched out into space and certain destruction. He'd devoted years to *Moonbreaker*. It must be like watching his child about to be blasted off into the nothingness beyond. She heard Nan trying to console her husband at the imminent loss of his beloved shuttle.

'It's over, love,' she said to him. 'It's done its job.

It got us here.'

'But . . . it's too soon,' he said, taking her hand.

'Isn't it always?' said Nan, as they looked deep into one another's eyes, sad smiles mirrored in each of their faces. Rod immediately softened and gave Indy a gentle kiss on the cheek. Nan was the best.

Vi's heart froze.

Nan.

The medicine.

Nan's medicine was still under her seat aboard *Moonbreaker*.

'No!' cried Vi, her turn to start hammering on the doors. 'It can't go! It can't!'

'It's OK, sweetie,' said Easter, trying to pull her into a hug. 'We'll find another way.'

'No – you don't understand,' said Vi, shaking off her mum and trying to prise the doors open with her bare hands. 'There's something on there, something important – I have to get inside!'

But Vi's efforts were hopeless. The doors were locked tight and the rumble of *Moonbreaker*'s rocket thrusters was getting ever louder. From the window next to the airlock, she could only watch as *Moonbreaker* prepared to launch.

'Shall we all count down together?' Umbra taunted. '*Five . . . four . . . three . . . two . . . one . . . LIFT OFF!*'

And with several deafening roars – one from *Moonbreaker* and another from Rod and Vi – the space shuttle that had brought them safely to NIDUS blasted into space without them, on a one-way journey to nowhere.

'OK,' panted Vi, her brain whirring with possibilities, 'this is a huge space station, right? There must be a way – maybe we could hack into *Moonbreaker* from here and guide it back? Or does this thing have a tractor beam, like I-Dem did, that can drag it towards us? Or do they have a space suit and we can fly out to it and fly back? Or—'

She felt Indy's hand on her shoulder and it immediately brought tears to her eyes.

'Let it go, love,' Indy whispered. 'You have to let it go.'

'I can't,' said Vi, tears winding down her face as she watched Nan's last hope drift off into space. 'I just can't.'

'Sure you can,' said Nan, giving her a big squeeze. 'You just don't know it yet.'

'But . . . I found it!' Vi insisted. 'I found a

medicine that could save you! On I-Dem! It would have made everything better!'

Indy took her granddaughter's hand in hers and kissed it gently.

'You don't know that,' she said with a warm smile. 'You can't save everyone, remember. And some of us don't need to be saved.'

'But . . . but . . . the medicine . . . it would have cured you,' Vi sniffed.

'Until the next thing,' Nan began. 'And the thing after that. And where's the magic medicine going to come from then? I'm seventy-nine years old, Vi. I've lived a wonderful life and now it's my time. Enjoy the rest of it with me, hey? Please?'

Vi looked into the pleading eyes of her grand-mother. She hated it with every fibre of her being. But she knew Indy was right. She nodded her head gently.

'Atta girl,' whispered Indy with another hug.

Vi looked over to where George and Robert were comforting a brooding Rod.

'Well, now,' said Umbra, her evil leer radiating from the nearest screen. 'Looks like you're here to stay. I'd love to chat some more, but the phone is ringing off the hook with offers for the Neurotrol

– which, by the way, is successfully uploaded into the NIDUS mainframe, so you're already too late. While those fools are running around down there trying to get me my money – and we know just how crummy government pay is, right, Easter? – I'm dealing with the real bidders. The ones who really, really want to be able to control the world. So I'd better not keep them waiting. I'll be seeing you, Easter Day. And I'll be ready.'

The screens flickered off, leaving the family in quiet despair in the corridor. Despite his outburst, Rod was the first to regroup.

'The plan is unchanged,' he growled quietly. 'Now, more than ever, we need to secure *Spinneret*, it's our only ride home. Find it, lock it down, make sure that maniac can't get to it.'

'Done and done,' said Robert gravely.

'You heard what she said, Lotus Flower,' said Rod, accepting Indy's hug. 'She's uploaded the chip. NIDUS *is* the Neurotrol. The only way to stop it is to blow this baby back to the Bronze Age.'

'Gotcha,' Nan nodded.

'Easter?' Rod asked.

'All over it,' said Vi's mum, looking as dangerous as she'd looked since Vi's last school report.

'Let's get to it,' said Rod. 'Everyone, accomplish your missions. And might I say, it's been an honour serving with you all.'

There was something about the finality of Rod's words that rocked Vi to her core. This was it. The big showdown. They either beat Umbra, or Umbra would destroy them. That was a lot for a twelve-year-old to take in. She looked at her mum, who softened at the sight of her little girl. Easter put down her weapon and took Vi in her arms.

'You be careful,' she said, her voice trembling with emotion.

'You too,' said Vi, squeezing both her eyes and her mother. What if this was the last time she held her? No, she couldn't think like that. Agent Lynx was the best in the business. Umbra stood no chance. 'I love you, Mum.'

'Love you most,' said Easter back, kissing Vi's head before releasing her and returning to spy mode.

'We rendezvous back at *Spinneret* ASAP,' said Rod, revving his mobility scooter. 'Good luck, everyone.'

'Good luck!' they all said to one another. As she

ran in search of their only ride home, Vi took a deep breath, regrouped and got her spy game on.

It was time to save the world.

Again.

'Where are they?' Agent Money asked, looking nervously at her watch. 'We're running out of time.'

'They'll be here,' promised The Wolf, with a confidence he didn't feel. Money was right. The clock was against them.

He pulled out his phone, which was feeding him images from the secret camera he had hidden inside Ragnarok ground control. He was a spy – what did anyone expect?

The Wolf watched the general pacing the floor nervously. That was a good sign, at least – the phone call hadn't come. And so long as his plan worked before that phone rang, he could still turn this thing around.

'Sir, do you think they can do it?' Agent Money asked nervously. 'Agent Lynx and her family, I mean? Can they really stop Umbra?'

The Wolf surprised himself with the strength of his reply.

'Yes,' he said simply. 'We just have to buy them the time to do it.'

Isaac looked back at his screen.

'We have reports coming in of massive disorder on a global scale,' a soldier reported to the general. 'People are fighting, looting, burning . . . Every government in the world is in chaos.'

'Does anyone know about Umbra and NIDUS?' the general asked.

'Negative,' the soldier replied. 'We have successfully contained the intelligence. For now.'

'Good.' The general wasn't alone in breathing a sigh of relief. Isaac knew that the last thing this situation needed was any more angry world leaders with itchy trigger fingers. The longer NIDUS remained their secret, the better.

'What are your orders, sir?' the soldier asked.

'We wait,' the general commanded. 'We wait until—'

'General! General! I have Old Lady on line one!'

The general snapped to attention and strode to the nearest phone. He picked up the line, but immediately started to cough.

'Sorry, ma'am,' he apologized. 'Fly in my throat. Yes, that is still my assessment of the situation. The threat level to human life is critical and unacceptable. In my opinion, a preliminary strike is our only option . . . I accept . . . Ready to receive.'

The general waved for hush. Ground control fell silent. He looked to one of his soldiers and repeated the numbers being given to him down the line.

'Six, one, zero, nine, two, four – can you confirm? Thank you, ma'am. I will keep you updated.'

The general returned the phone and spun around to the soldier at the desk.

'Did you get that?'

'Yes, sir!' the soldier barked back. 'The codes have been accepted.'

A sickening smile crossed the general's lips.

'Prepare to fire on my command!' he barked. 'Launching missile in five . . . four . . . three . . .'

The tense air of ground control was suddenly punctured by the unmistakable sound of soft jazz.

'What . . . what's that?' the general yelled.

The Wolf smiled. He recognized it.

'Sir,' a trembling agent replied. 'I think – I think it's . . . a saxophone.'

'HOLD IT RIGHT THERE!' came the husky yell from the bridge, accompanied by the sound of several shotguns being fired in the air. 'EVERYONE, GET YOUR HANDS UP! I WANT TO SMELL YOUR ARMPITS LIKE IT'S THIRTY DEGREES AND YOU'RE WEARING LYCRA!'

'You 'eard ze lady!' came the second yell, also accompanied by gunfire. 'If you start ze working, I will start ze killing, *oui*?'

'Move aside, sucker!' the third yell rang out as the general's soldier was dispatched with an atomic wedgie. 'I'm missing horsey riding for this, so you'd better stay out of my way, or I'll make sure you NEVER win another level of Candy Crush ever again!'

'Oooh – love what you've done with the place,' came a fourth, more gentle voice. 'Reminds me of my old chiropodist's office – the one whose cousin moved to Burnley to start a landscaping business.'

The Wolf entered ground control and stood back to watch Silver Service and EVIL do their thing. He had to admire them – be it with bazookas or Battenberg, they had the whole room under control within minutes.

'What – WHAT IS THE MEANING OF THIS?!' the general blasted. 'YOU HAVE NO AUTHORITY HERE!'

The Wolf watched as Siren perched on a desk and cocked her rifle at General Bark.

'And I have no breath mints here,' she rasped. 'Looks like it's going to be a tough night for us all. Now get 'em up, GI Joe, or I'm gonna blow. And I ain't just talking about my gun.'

'This . . . this is . . . treason!' the general screamed. 'Umbra must be stopped!'

'And she will be – without the murder of seven innocent heroes,' said The Wolf, as the Silver Service tottered down and politely replaced the soldiers at their stations.

'Don't mind me,' whispered Reg, taking his spot at the main console. 'I have so much respect for you military personnel. Which reminds me, my great-uncle on my dad's sister's side served in World War Two. I mean, he served soup – he had a dicky bowel and shocking cataracts – but I feel such a connection with you people.'

'I told you,' The Wolf growled. 'Those are my people up there and I will protect them. From anyone.'

'You're too late,' the general snarled with a nasty smile. 'The codes have already been inputted. That system is encrypted with a triple A lock that took a team of one hundred cryptologists three years to encode. There's no way you can—'

'Done it,' sighed Missy, bursting a big gum bubble as she rolled her chair away from the computer and went back to playing on her phone.

The Wolf smiled back at the general.

'You were saying?' he said. 'Agent Money. Take the general somewhere he can be more . . . comfortable. I believe the downstairs lavatory is ideal.'

'Enjoy your moment,' the general hissed as Agent Money handcuffed his wrists. 'Because this is on you. We had a chance to stop this thing and you didn't take it. When this goes south, you will spend the rest of your days in a secure military facility with nothing but rats for company. And I'll be there to spit in your food.'

The Wolf and the general stared tensely at one another.

'*Bof*. Please let me kill ziz one,' Auguste pleaded. 'He has an 'ead just like ze butt.'

'Take him away,' The Wolf instructed, returning to the screen ahead.

'Reg, can you try to establish comms with our team?' he asked.

'Absolutely,' said Reg. 'It's so important to stay in touch. Which reminds me, I must call my old neighbour, Sita – she's been having a terrible time with her cladding.'

'Reg?' The Wolf prompted.

'Sorry!' giggled Reg. 'I'll see what I can do.'

As ground control returned to his command, The Wolf allowed himself a breath. The family were safe. He'd done his bit.

He just hoped to everything holy that they were ready to do theirs.

CHAPTER 15

'It's here!'

Vi allowed herself a small sigh of relief as the familiar sight of *Spinneret* came into view on the third docking bay they tried. Its white outsides had sustained some damage from their space battle and the black nose was a little bent. But it was there. And it could get them home. That was something, at least.

'Excellent,' said Robert, walking through the open airlock and on to the shuttle. 'That's one less thing to worry about.'

'Which brings our total to about seven million, six hundred thousand and ninety-six,' said Vi, going through the airlock with Russell and George. As she transferred between NIDUS and *Spinneret*, Vi looked out of the clear airlock side doors into the boundless darkness beyond – the same kind that had taken her out on her perilous spacewalk. Space was truly beautiful.

But she didn't fancy being stuck here.

They squeezed into the inside of *Spinneret*. It wasn't nearly as fancy – nor as big – as Rod's *Moonbreaker*, but she didn't care. So long as it got them out of there, that was all that mattered.

'Now, how do we lock this thing down so Umbra can't launch it?' George mused, sitting at the controls. 'The console is completely different to *Moonbreaker*.'

'Didn't this used to be a SPIDER shuttle?' Russell piped up, sitting down next to his dad.

'Yeah,' Vi confirmed, looking around for anything that might help. Or anything that she could eat – she was starving again. Space food didn't fill you up for very long. 'Rod said that they built it to shuttle astronauts to NIDUS.'

'Well, then,' said Russell, picking up a headset. 'Maybe we can contact SPIDER and get them to control it from the ground? We know Gumfoot was destroyed as a ground station—'

'Nearly taking you with it,' George said grimly.

'But the system must be preserved on a

cloud-based system somewhere,' Russell insisted. 'The Wolf should be able to access it. I mean, it's just a theory, but . . .'

'You are brilliant,' said George proudly. 'And absolutely right. We know the comms work on here — we had that unpleasant encounter with Umbra after all — so if we can just contact ground control . . .'

Russell fiddled with a few buttons on the deck before speaking into his headset.

'Ground control? Come in, ground control? This is Russell Sprout aboard *Spinneret*. Are you receiving me?'

The unwelcome, but not unfamiliar sound of static returned his call. Vi tried to steady her heartbeat. They were going to be OK. Really.

'Ground control? I repeat — ground control?' Russell announced, fiddling with the dials on the dashboard. 'We have control of *Spinneret* and request urgent assistance. Can you read me?'

The crackle crackled back.

Vi felt her stomach lurch. They were all alone.

But Russell Sprout wasn't giving up. Vi hoped, if they ever escaped this, he'd always be her techie. He was the absolute best.

'I'm going to try the emergency frequency,' Russell said, his hands a blur across the flight deck. 'So long as someone picks up, maybe we can get hold of them?'

'Another great idea,' George beamed, turning a dial around and listening in on his headset.

'This is Russell Sprout, calling aboard *Spinneret*, do you—'

'Russell? Agent Sprout – is that you? Urgent confirmation required!'

Vi tried not to scream out. That was The Wolf. They had made contact.

'Yes! Yes – it's us!' Russell nearly squealed. 'Thank goodness we found you!'

'Urgent situation report requested,' The Wolf commanded. 'We tracked *Moonbreaker*, but could detect no personnel on board. We feared Umbra had you trapped.'

'Just let her try,' said Robert confidently, winking at Vi. She wished she shared his swagger. But she was glad she didn't share his cheesiness.

'Easter – Agent Lynx – is in pursuit of Umbra. Agents Redback and Labyrinth are accessing the Doomsday switch,' Russell reported. 'Our primary mission is to secure *Spinneret* for our transit back to Earth — *Moonbreaker* is down, I repeat, *Moonbreaker* is down. Are you able to override the system to secure *Spinneret* to be launched manually on our command? We believe that the protocol will be stored in the . . .'

Vi zoned out as Russell reeled off the technobabble that he and SPIDER spoke so fluently. She caught her father looking intently at her.

'You OK, darling?' Robert asked. 'This is an awful lot for your young shoulders to be carrying.'

'I'm fine,' Vi slightly lied. 'But I'm really hungry.'

'Me too,' Robert grinned. 'Er, George — if you and the boy wonder have it nailed down here, Vi and I might go back into NIDUS in search of some supplies. An army marches on its stomach, after all . . .'

'Good idea,' George smiled. 'I believe we passed a kitchen module about two hundred and forty-seven metres to the left. But it could have been as few as two hundred and forty-three . . .'

'I'll try both,' Robert said, gesturing for Vi to lead the way through the airlock that would take them back into the main space station. 'Any special requests?'

'Coffee,' said George. He looked super-tired.

'Chocolate,' said Russell, who looked just like he always did. Russell was nothing if not reliable. And that was what this situation really needed.

'Roger that,' said Robert, following Vi into the open airlock. 'I just hope they have a drinks cabinet on board. I could murder a—'

The doors on both sides of the airlock suddenly snapped shut, trapping Robert and Vi between NIDUS and *Spinneret*. Vi pressed around the clear walls. They were stuck, suspended in this clear box in space.

'Well, hello again,' came the grim voice of Umbra over the sound system. 'Now, what do you think you're doing with my rocket? Didn't anyone ever tell you it's not right to steal?'

'Scotland Yard, Interpol and every law enforcement agency south of the Arctic Circle, now you mention it,' Robert quipped. 'What do you want, Umbra?'

'Well, Sir Charge – Robert – now you mention it, I've been feeling for some time that I really do owe you one. All those years of loyal service . . . I'm here to help family relations,' Umbra continued. 'I sensed a bit of tension between you and Sprout there – thought I might be able to help.'

'George and I are great friends now, thank you for asking,' Robert replied. 'If you're going to worry about friendships, I suggest you start with your own. Easter is on her way. And I'm not sure she's in a very forgiving mood.'

'Well, quite – and I don't think it's because I never returned her casserole dish,' Umbra glowered. 'But I can kill two birds with one stone here. Three, in fact. You betrayed me, Robert. I've been biding my time, but I'm afraid as your employer, I can't let that pass. And I need to knock Easter off her A-game . . . so I thought you and your darling daughter might enjoy a little spacewalk together.'

Vi felt her guts twist. The spacewalk with George had nearly killed them both. And she was in no rush to repeat it.

'You're a butthead,' Vi shot back, noting again her need to work on her smart spy comebacks.

'Be that as it may – I've been very busy lately, what with one thing and another,' her former godmother continued darkly. 'And – silly Aunty Honey – I quite forgot to leave you some space suits. So when I blast you out of that airlock in thirty seconds' time, you might feel a bit of a chill.'

Vi's internal panic was mirrored in her father's face. Space had been dangerous enough with the suits. Without them, they'd die in seconds.

The airlock suddenly turned red. She watched George and Russell spring from their seats and jab the button to open the door. But it was locked fast. The all-too-familiar timer flashed up at thirty seconds. Nan had said that life was a ticking clock. But Vi was getting pretty sick of them ticking down her own life.

'Easter? Easter, my dear?' Umbra announced. 'If you're listening, I've got good news and bad. The good news is that in thirty seconds' time, you won't need to worry about that idiot ex-husband of yours. The less good news is that you'll never see your only child again. But you have to take the rough with the smooth.'

'Honey!' came Easter's furious voice across the microphone. Vi smiled. Now Umbra was in trouble. Easter Day had found her. And she wasn't going to let her get away a second time. 'This ends NOW!' Easter shouted. 'Robert? Are you both OK?'

'Easter – you stay on mission,' Robert

commanded. 'I've got this.'

Vi looked around the empty airlock.

'Got this how?' Vi whispered.

'Trust me,' Robert winked, but even his smug confidence seemed a little uncertain.

'I mean it, Honey!' Easter raged. 'This is your one chance to surrender!'

'I see. I'm afraid, rather like with your curried goat haggis – I'm going to have to pass,' Umbra retorted.

'I'm warning you, Honey,' Easter threatened.

'I'm so sorry, you two – I need to take care of a little . . . irritation. Do have fun. And Vi?'

'What?' Vi snapped, trying to sound brave against the screams of worry in her brain.

'You know when I said you were the best singer in your school Christmas concert?'

'What about it?'

'I lied,' Umbra growled. 'Goodbye, Valentine Day.'

There was a brief, fevered grunting of fighting, then the microphone went dead.

Vi looked at George banging at the airlock doors from inside *Spinneret*. The timer started to count down.

'Is there something you can smash it with?' Robert called.

'Negative,' George replied, jabbing again at the release button. 'If these doors aren't secure, then when Umbra opens the airlock, we'll all be sucked into space. We have to open them and get you safely behind them.'

'Agent Wolf? Agent Wolf?' Vi heard Russell calling urgently down the intercom. 'Urgent assistance required. Manual override for Airlock Three needed critically. Do you copy?'

'Cool your jets, dummy,' came a rude, but very welcome voice over the intercom. 'I'm already on it. Override code incoming.'

'Missy Fit?' Vi exclaimed. 'What's she doing there?'

'Robert? Robert?' came a rasping voice, accompanied by some sad jazz. 'We're here. We have control. We have breath mints. Everything's going to be OK.'

'Siren,' said Robert. 'Siren – if anything happens to me ...'

'It won't,' Siren promised. 'I'd bet my last nose hair on it.'

'But if it does,' Robert continued, 'I want you

to know that . . . I love you. I want to spend the rest of my life with you. Even if that's only . . . twenty-two seconds.'

'Oh, Robbie,' Siren breathed. 'I love you too. Like a girl loves her waxing strips. Stay strong, we're going to get you out of there. Dave? Something a little more upbeat, please?'

The jazz soundtrack changed to a tense beat.

'Missy?' Russell said urgently, hitting the keys on the dashboard. 'I'm going to need that code.'

'Come along, Missy, help the nice people facing certain death in the airlock,' came the calm voice of Missy's mother.

'CAN IT, JANET!' Missy screamed back. 'It's like I told you at Parental Respect Class – shut up and let me do what I want!'

Vi looked at the timer. Eighteen seconds. She felt her dad's arms around her.

'It's going to be OK,' he said bravely. 'I've got you.'

There was a horrible silence as they waited for the codes that would free them, time moving both too quickly and too slowly. Russell raced to the keypad and stood, poised for the numbers. Vi watched the clock ticking down. *Fifteen* . . .

fourteen . . . thirteen . . .

'Do you know, this reminds me of the time my bridge partner, Gladys, got stuck in a portaloo on Southend Pier,' Vi heard Reg chipping in. 'It took two fire brigades and a whole tub of margarine to get her out.'

'Nearly there,' yawned Missy.

Vi watched the timer. *Eleven . . . ten . . . nine . . .*

'GOT IT!' Missy shouted out. 'Six, five, eight, nine, two, three.'

Russell punched the code into the keypad and the airlock doors to NIDUS and *Spinneret* opened. Vi felt Robert push her out into NIDUS's circular corridor. She was safe. She and her dad were—

'Robert!' she heard George shout as the NIDUS door suddenly snapped shut behind her.

'What's happening?' Russell shouted down his headset.

'The system is fighting my hack,' Missy called back. 'I can override it again, but it'll take time.'

'We don't have time! Russell – close the *Spinneret* door!' Robert shouted back in a strangled tone. 'Now!'

Vi spun around. Her dad was stuck on the

opposite side of the glass to her.

And trapped between the doors . . . was his tie.

'DAD!' she screamed, desperately trying to prise the doors apart. There were only seconds left until the space doors opened and Robert would be exposed to the deadly conditions outside. Robert tried to reach his tie knot. But the doors had slammed right at the top of his tie, trapping him in a position that meant he could neither see what he was doing, nor get his arms to the right angle to free himself.

'Dad?' Russell asked George, his fingers hovering over the button to close the *Spinneret* airlock door. 'What do I do?'

'Get ready to shut that door,' boomed George. 'No one gets left behind.'

Vi looked at her stepfather again.

Wow, did he know how to do a hero moment.

Without a millisecond's hesitation, George Sprout threw himself into the airlock, throwing his arms around Robert and working at the tie with lightning fingers.

'Damn these Oxford knots,' he muttered.

'Dad?' said Russell anxiously. 'Dad . . . we have five seconds.'

'On my command, you close those doors,' George ordered, working the first loop of Robert's tie free. 'You ready?'

'Ready,' Russell confirmed.

'GO!' yelled George.

The next few seconds were such a blur, it took Vi a moment to piece them all together. Practically within the same heartbeat, George undid Robert's tie, freeing him from the NIDUS doors while Russell punched in the code to close the *Spinneret* ones. With two seconds on the timer, George grabbed Robert around the waist and yanked him back inside *Spinneret*, just as the doors to the spacecraft closed – and a split second before the doors to space opened.

It all happened in under two seconds. But they were the longest two seconds of Vi's life.

'Dad! George! Are you OK?' she shouted at the panting heap of parents on the floor over the other side of the airlock.

For a moment, neither of them moved, George lying underneath Robert like a koala on a eucalyptus tree as Robert's tie froze and withered in the unforgiving atmosphere in space. Vi gulped. That could have been them.

'Er, George old boy?' came Robert's first utterance.

'Yeah?' panted George.

'Do you think you could, you know, let me go?' Robert asked politely.

'Oh, gosh ... yes, of course,' said George, releasing his arms, before Robert rolled off and helped him to his feet.

They dusted themselves down, before their eyes met in an awkward pause.

'How did you do that?' Russell asked breathlessly.

'Boy Scouts,' said George proudly. 'Knot-tying champion. I still hold the 12th West Wittering Troop record for the fastest Trucker's Hitch.'

'George . . . I . . . don't know what to say,' Robert stuttered.

'It's nothing,' said George. 'You would have done the same.'

There was an awkward pause where no one pointed out that, actually, Robert had already proven he would have done precisely the opposite.

But it seemed a shame to ruin the moment.

'You're a good man,' said Robert. 'Thank you

for having my back. Sincerely.'

'Any time,' said George, giving him a manly hug. 'I know you'll have mine too.'

'Any time,' Robert repeated, gratefully returning the embrace.

'Er, when you've all finished the latest instalment of *Saps in Space*,' Missy interrupted, 'you might want to know that I've locked *Spinneret*'s launch codes. She's not going anywhere unless you say.'

'Thanks, Missy,' said Russell, smiling as Robert offered a sobbing George his hankie.

Vi looked on with happy relief. That was one feud dealt with. She looked up the corridor to where she could hear Easter and Honey fighting.

'Vi!' Robert called out. 'You stay there. Your mother's got this.'

Vi nodded at her dad. Of course Easter had this. She was the best of the best.

She was also Vi's mum.

'Er . . . sorry, Dad. I'll see you in a bit. Gotta go,' Vi half-apologized as she sprinted up the corridor.

'VALENTINE DAY, GET BACK HERE!' she heard her father roar.

But Vi had already gone.

Easter Day might be the best of the best.

But even the best needed a bit of support sometimes.

CHAPTER 16

Easter Day had waited a long time for this day. The last time she had faced Umbra – or what she had believed was the last time – she thought she had defeated the world's most wanted super-villain. This time, she needed to be sure. That was over ten years ago. But today she was also fighting her best friend, Honey B, godmother to her only child. She had to push those thoughts away. Honey B was a lie. Umbra was the truth behind her – and Umbra had to be stopped. It was time to finish what she had started all those years ago. Easter remembered every moment of how it had felt to fight Umbra before, as if it were yesterday.

'Ouch!' she cried as she took a roundhouse kick to her head.

But she had forgotten quite how much it hurt.

'Had enough?' Umbra taunted, her fists raised as she prepared for another onslaught.

'Never!' Easter spat back, although in truth, she could have done with a five-minute breather.

She looked around the circular room for anything that could help her. They were in the very heart of NIDUS, the round nerve centre that controlled the whole space station. On the screens to her left, Easter could see the chaos that the Neurotrol was already unleashing on Earth. Out of the airlock to her right, she could see the world that she was trying to save. By the end of this fight, only one of those outcomes would remain.

'Do you remember that day?' Umbra asked, ducking and weaving to disorientate her opponent.

'How could I forget?' Easter replied, her own fists raised in defence. 'It's not every day you back-flip across a room and ninja-kick your sworn enemy into piranha-infested waters in an exploding power station. Although, in fairness, it was the third time that month. I'm curious, Honey. However did you survive?'

Easter launched a spinning kick of her own, but Umbra nimbly ducked out of the way. She was quicker and – if Easter was entirely honest – stronger. Easter was going to have to fight smart.

Umbra shrugged.

'I'm an excellent swimmer,' she said smugly. 'And contrary to popular perception, piranhas rarely attack humans. Unless they are an aggressive mutant strain, of course.'

Easter knew this all too well after she had rehoused several in her garden pond, only for them to eat her koi carp, then next door's cat, then each other. She wished she had George here to give her some kind of geeky fact about piranhas. In fact, she wished George were just here at all.

'I'm so sorry about Vi,' Umbra taunted. 'But the good thing about death in space is at least it's quick. If I'd had my way, I'd have made her – and you – suffer much more.'

Easter fought the pounding in her chest. Was Vi all right? An image of her little girl in the deathly conditions outside swayed Easter for a critical moment – had Umbra really taken her little girl away?

No.

Easter would know. Her heart would be

broken. There was no way that Robert, George and Russell would have allowed that to happen. After a life spent fighting, Easter Day knew that there was one thing no weapon could touch – love. And Vi was shielded by it on all sides. Her daughter was alive, Easter knew it in the core of her being as only a mother can. Umbra was trying to get in her head. Easter had to focus on defeating her . . .

'OUCH!' she cried again, as Umbra took advantage of her distraction to land another massive blow on Easter's chest, knocking her across the room.

'Come on, Easter – this is embarrassing,' Umbra laughed. 'This is supposed to be the epic showdown, the ultimate battle of good versus evil. I've seen more fight in a January sale.'

Easter rose to her feet and tried to push her daughter out of her mind. Her mission was here. She had to accomplish it. And she would.

Just as soon as she caught her breath.

'So you survived the power station?' she asked Umbra, the two of them circling the room. 'Then what?'

"Well, then, I needed somewhere to hide until I could take revenge on you,' said Umbra, crouching down like a panther. 'Of course, I thought I still had Robert on side, but it seems as though everyone in your family is a disappointment to me.'

Easter launched across the room and landed a flying kick, knocking Honey against the opposite wall.

'Don't disrespect my family,' she said, as the super-villain wiped a small trickle of blood from the side of her mouth.

'Touchy much?' Umbra whispered. 'It was pathetically easy, actually. The Blacksmith – Walter – forged me a complete identity as Honey B and I joined SPIDER so I could watch you all. Of course, you decided to be a full-time mum not long after I joined – you never really did have the heart for this, did you? Nor the skills.'

A swift punch from Easter quickly suggested otherwise. Easter watched her former best friend snarl as she wiped her nose. She was getting to her. Good.

'Although, I couldn't just kill you on your way to the shops – where's the poetry in that?' Umbra continued, circling the room again. 'I needed to get into your life. Your mind. Your heart. That way, when you found out exactly how stupid you had been, it would break you completely.'

Easter flipped across the room and propelled herself at Umbra with a flying kick, sending her opponent crashing against the window.

'Guess again, Umbra,' said Easter, springing back to her feet and raising her fists. She tried to control her ragged breathing as Honey wiped her bleeding mouth and pulled herself to her feet. She was starting to look tired. Easter drew strength from that.

'I'm so sorry to hear that your mother won't be with us for very much longer,' Umbra smiled. Easter fought hard to quell the rage burning in her stomach. She wasn't going to let Honey get to her. She wouldn't give her the satisfaction. 'Although, ironically, she might just outlive you – if only for a few moments. In fact, it might be fun to have her watch me destroy her only child. Just like I destroyed yours.'

'Mum!' came the most welcome voice in the world.

'Vi!' said Easter, seeing her beautiful daughter appear in the doorway behind them. Her whole body breathed a sigh of relief. Vi was OK. She felt her soul recharge.

'What can I do?' Vi cried.

'Stay with your dads,' Easter commanded. 'And stay alive. Mummy needs to kick Umbra's butt.'

'I want to help.'

'Valentine!' Easter snapped. 'Go back to the family. I've got this.'

'Darling, we have control of *Spinneret*!' George announced over the intercom. 'So when you're . . . er . . . finished, meet us here so we can go home!'

'Copy that,' said Easter. 'I love you, baby.'

'I love you more.'

'I love you most.'

'Like chocolate toast,' they said together.

'Eeeeeuuuuurgh,' exclaimed Honey, gagging on her own words. 'Enough! If I wasn't going to kill you before, you'd better believe I will now! Easter Day, it's time to DIE!!!'

Easter watched as Umbra launched herself across the room. She was a ferocious opponent. But Easter had beaten her before. And she was going to beat her again.

'AAAAAAAARRRRRRGGGGHHH!' she screamed, sprinting across the room to launch her counter-attack. Easter Day didn't wait for the fight to come to her.

She brought it.

Every. Single. Time.

'Well, that was close,' chuckled Reg back at mission control. 'I was so tense I nearly crushed my dentures! Which reminds me . . .'

'Any news on Easter and Umbra?' The Wolf interrupted. There was a time and place for Reg's anecdotes. Neither was now.

'There's frantic movement in the control room,' Agent Money reported, looking at her tracking device. 'But more than that? I just don't know.'

The Wolf nodded imperceptibly. Easter was alive. And that was all she needed to remain.

'Oi!' came a voice over the intercom. 'Anyone there?'

'Agent Labyrinth?' Isaac replied. 'What's your status?'

'Bloomin' uncomfortable,' Indy grumbled. 'Aren't you done yet?'

'Almost there, Lotus Flower,' came Rod's loving growl in reply. 'Wolf. Can you confirm the location of the Doomsday switch?'

The Wolf summoned up the NIDUS schematics on the screen.

'I can,' Isaac replied. 'It is to the left of the rotary switch, behind the remote activation switch. If you flick the switch to green, it should be armed.'

There was a series of undignified groans.

'Done!' Rod announced triumphantly. 'It's on. Are you receiving the activation signal?'

The Wolf looked at his screen. It was blank. That wasn't good.

'Not receiving,' he replied. 'Try again.'

He heard Rod flick the switch a second time.

'And now?' Rod asked.

'Nothing. Yet,' The Wolf replied with false optimism, a lurching fear growing in his stomach. 'One more time?'

For a third time, he heard Rod flick the switch. They waited. And waited. And waited.

For a third time, nothing happened.

'Anything?'

The Wolf tried to frame a positive response.

But there wasn't one.

'No,' he said eventually. 'I'm so sorry, Agent Redback.'

There was a long and heavy silence.

'Don't be,' sighed Rod eventually. 'Leave this with us. I'll report back.'

The signal immediately went dead.

'What was all that about?' Siren asked. 'Is it all working? Everything OK?'

The Wolf didn't know how to respond. But everything was most definitely not OK.

'The Doomsday switch is working,' he said. 'But the remote activation is not.'

Silence greeted his words. He had no idea if that was because everyone understood what that meant, or because no one did.

'So what?' Missy clarified.

'So,' said Isaac heavily, 'we can't destroy NIDUS from down here.'

'And?' said Missy impatiently.

'And that means that it has to be activated manually,' Siren sighed. Clearly she understood exactly what that meant.

'I don't get it,' said Missy, sucking loudly on her lolly. 'What's the big deal?'

'The big deal?' The Wolf replied. 'The big deal is that if they are going to destroy NIDUS, one of them is going to have to stay behind to do it.'

Vi watched, powerless, as her mum and Umbra battled their way around the control room. She didn't care what her mum said, she wasn't going anywhere, not if there was a chance she could help. If Umbra was hurting, she was showing no signs. Vi knew that meant Easter Day wasn't going to show any either.

'Not bad for an OAP,' grinned Honey, standing on one leg and launching a series of jabbing kicks at Easter with the other. 'But how long can you keep this up?'

'How long have you got?' growled Easter, grabbing Honey's leg and forcing her into a backflip to escape.

They stood across from one another again. Vi observed a slight wince as Honey got off the floor. Perhaps she was hurting after all.

'I don't suppose I could interest you in a deal?' the super-villain asked smoothly. 'After all, I'm about to come into a bit of money. I believe the current bid is three hundred trillion dollars. The smallest fraction of that could buy you and the family a luxurious life anywhere you wanted. I'm thinking of buying Hawaii . . .'

'Never,' said Easter. 'Maybe your human decency can be bought. Mine isn't for sale.'

Vi felt her heart swell with pride at her mum's morality.

Although Hawaii did sound nice.

'Use your brain, Easter,' Honey advised. 'After all, your body isn't what it used to be.'

Easter cartwheeled over to Umbra, kicked her feet out from underneath her and was about to pin her down when Umbra flipped up and flicked across the room to safety. Now it was Vi's turn to wince. Her mum was so cool. But even she couldn't keep this up for ever.

'My body's just fine, thanks,' said Easter, raising her arms for another attack. 'I'd be far more concerned about yours, if I were you.'

'Last chance,' Umbra goaded. 'I'm offering you the chance of a life of unparalleled luxury – indeed, I'm offering you the chance of a life. All you have to do is stand down. Let me get what I'm owed and we all return to Earth alive and rich beyond all measure. Otherwise, when I inevitably defeat you, I'm going to tie you to a chair and make you watch as I launch your family members out of that airlock and into space, one by one. I'll even let you push the button for Robert – to make up for the casserole dish.'

Vi ignored the fluttering in her heart. There was nothing Easter wouldn't do to keep her family safe. But sell out to Umbra and leave the world at the mercy of whichever maniac bought the Neurotrol? Vi knew that just couldn't happen. But how could Vi help her?

'I'm going to give you one more chance to surrender,' Vi's mum snarled. 'Then I'm going to whoop your butt and get it back down to Earth to face justice for your crimes.'

'Oh, Easter,' sighed Umbra as they circled the deck. 'Easter, Easter, Easter. You always were a fool. You were a fool when you eloped with Robert. You were a fool when you thought you could defeat me. You were a fool when you fell for the Honey B routine. And you're a fool for sentencing your entire family to death. You could have saved them, Easter. Remember that.'

'And you could have saved yourself,' Easter replied, glancing at the airlock behind her that could launch her family into space. 'Remember that.'

Umbra suddenly sprinted across the room again, but this time, Easter wasn't ready for her. Undecided how to brace herself for the next onslaught, she ended up unbalanced and unprepared. Umbra was too good a fighter not to exploit her opponent's indecision and, with a fearful roar, kicked Easter's arm hard against the airlock door. Vi heard a sickening crack in her mum's wrist as Easter crumpled to the floor. Her cuss confirmed what Vi feared – her mum had a broken arm. And with an injury like that, there was no way Easter could defeat Umbra.

Umbra stood in the middle of the room, panting. But then a sickening smile crossed her face. She stalked towards Easter, who was sitting on the floor holding her wrist, a defiant grimace on her face doing a bad job of disguising her pain.

'Oh dear,' said Umbra, running a finger down Easter's face. 'Looks like it's game over, Agent Lynx.'

'Go to hell,' Easter spat.

Umbra tutted.

'Now that's no way to speak in front of the children,' she said, standing and walking towards Vi, who was frozen to the spot with fear. Half of her wanted to run from Umbra. But there was no way she was leaving her mum.

Umbra continued her slow prowl towards Vi. Her body was screaming at her to move. But she couldn't. And as Umbra grabbed her by the hair, she was denied the choice.

'YOU PUT HER DOWN!' Easter cried, struggling to her feet with the help of her one good arm.

'Now,' said Umbra loudly over the sounds of Vi's screaming as she was dragged by her hair to the airlock. 'Let's leave the boys out of this – I'll deal with them later. For old times' sake, I'm going to give you the choice. Easter – do you want me to launch Vi into space while you watch? Or shall we let Vi watch as I do it to you? In the interests of fairness, I will say that you'll both end up out there anyway, but what kind of friend would I be if I didn't offer you the alternatives?'

Easter looked squarely at Vi.

'Remember your nan's advice,' she whispered, glancing over Vi's shoulder as Umbra pulled her past.

Vi stared intently at her mum. What was she trying to tell her? Nan had loads of advice: *don't wear your coat indoors if you want to feel the benefit; if the wind changes you'll stay like that; always wear clean underwear in case you end up in an ambulance—*

A spy's greatest weapon is their mind.

That's what Mum needed Vi to do. She needed to fight with her head. But how?

'Me first,' Easter said, standing tall in front of the airlock. 'Vi – turn around, I don't want you to see this.'

Vi's head tried to wrestle with her panicking heart as she turned away. She couldn't believe her mum was going to do this. Easter was trying to show her something. But what?

'Oh, no, no, no,' said Umbra, turning Vi back so she was directly facing the airlock. 'You're going to watch every second of your mother's death, Ms Valentine. And then you can go and join her.'

'You'll regret the day you ever threatened my child,' Easter growled. 'I swear it, Umbra.'

'If you say so,' Umbra smiled, hitting the button to open the airlock. 'So, shall we get this over and done with? If you'll forgive my nostalgia, a back-flip across the room with a ninja-kick should do the trick.'

'Ready when you are,' Easter promised, standing firm in the open doorway.

'Mum — no!' Vi cried. She couldn't believe that Easter was going down without a fight. She couldn't lose her mum. She couldn't. Easter's eyes were flicking frantically to her left — what was she trying to say?!

'Easter Day! This ends now!' Umbra roared. 'Right now! AAAAAAARRRRRGGGGGH-HHH!'

Umbra began her backflips across the room. Vi watched as she charged towards her mum, tearing up the distance between them. Any moment now, she'd kick Easter into the airlock and that would be the end of—

The airlock.

With a gasp, Vi suddenly realized what her mum was asking her to do. She started to creep towards the button, hoping Umbra couldn't see through her acrobatics. She wasn't close enough. Easter glanced over and winked. She was ready. Vi edged closer, closer, closer . . .

'Get ready,' Easter whispered as she gathered her broken arm into her body. 'Hold it, hold it, hold it . . .'

Vi could feel her muscles twitching. One wrong move and they were both dead. She couldn't mess this up. For their sakes, or the rest of the world.

'NOW!' Easter screamed. Within a second, everything happened. As Umbra began her flying leap towards Easter, with her last ounce of strength, Vi's mum dived out of Umbra's way, rolling beneath the flying super-villain with a bone-shaking thud. With no Easter to stop her, Umbra flew into the open airlock as Easter howled on the floor. Knowing she had only heartbeats before Umbra regrouped, Vi launched herself headlong at the airlock button to close her inside. With all her might, Vi leapt the few metres between her and the button, punching it hard as she flew past and landing painfully on the ground beyond.

For a moment, Vi lay, dazed, on the floor, hoping beyond hope that her flying leap had hit the mark. Had she actually made contact with the button? She almost didn't want to look to find out. Failure was absolutely not an option right now. The safety of the world depended on that one moment . . .

But a fevered slamming on the airlock doors quickly sent a flood of relief through Vi's terrified body. She turned around to see exactly what she had hoped.

Umbra was trapped inside the airlock.

They'd got her. They'd won.

'Easter! Easter! Are you OK?' came George's terrified voice over the system. 'Please let me know what's going on!'

Easter let out a deep breath. Then quickly drew it back in again. Vi figured she really needed the oxygen.

'I'm fine,' Easter said, wincing as she lifted her broken wrist. 'The situation is contained. Umbra is in our custody. It's over.'

Vi's ears stung with the whooping and cheering that came across the system. But it also brought a smile to her face. She raced over to her mum and threw herself into Easter's arms.

'WE DID IT!' Vi screamed in joy.

'OWWWWWW!' Easter screamed in agony.

'Oh – ooops – sorry!' Vi winced as her mum brought herself carefully up to standing, cradling her broken wrist.

'It's OK, baby,' Easter smiled. 'Everything is

274

going to be OK now.'

They stood there, holding gratefully on to one another. But the insistent banging next to them brought the touching moment to a quick close. Inside the airlock, all of Umbra's composure had been lost to her defeat. She was flailing and gnashing like a caged animal, hammering and clawing at the airlock doors with her hands and nails.

'There's no point,' Easter said calmly to Umbra. 'You're trapped. We've got you. You lost. We're taking you back to Earth.'

Umbra stopped her thrashing. For a few seconds, she stood panting in the airlock, her head hanging down, her fists clenched. Then she raised her head. And her dark eyes met Easter's, filled with the hate of a thousand feuds.

'I never lose,' she growled. 'And you're not taking me anywhere.'

'Face it, Honey,' Easter said calmly. 'You're out of time and you're out of options. The second we get out of here, SPIDER is going to blow this place sky-high. The Neurotrol will be destroyed. And you will be put somewhere you can never cause trouble again.'

'Yeah. Exactly,' said Vi, really, really wishing she

had something cooler to say.

But instead of anger or fear, a twisted smile formed on Umbra's face.

'I wouldn't be so sure about that,' she teased. 'I made a few . . . adjustments to the Doomsday switch when I got here. A little insurance policy. Just in case.'

'What do you mean?' Easter demanded.

'What's wrong with it?' Vi asked.

'Oh, you'll find out,' Umbra smirked. 'And how you'd just love to take me in, wouldn't you? Easter Day – the big hero who brought Umbra to justice. Well, I hate to disappoint you, Agent Lynx. But it's just not going to happen. Not today. Not ever.'

Umbra peeled herself away from the doors and swayed casually over to the opposite side of the airlock, to the space doors.

Right over to the exit button.

She stroked it with her middle finger, circling it lovingly.

'Umbra – Honey – don't be so stupid,' Easter warned. 'You go out there, you'll be dead within seconds.'

'Is that so?' said Umbra, looking like she was

thinking about it. 'Oh, well, then . . .'

And with a twisted grin, she pushed the button.

'*AIRLOCK ENGAGED,*' the NIDUS computer voice intoned. '*AIRLOCK OPENING IN THIRTY SECONDS. TWENTY-NINE . . . TWENTY-EIGHT . . . TWENTY-SEVEN . . .*'

Vi's guts clenched. This wasn't how this was supposed to go.

'Honey, stop it!' Easter shouted. 'Stop it now! You'll die!'

'I'm dead already!' Umbra cried, throwing her hands in the air. 'You know what'll happen to me down there! There isn't a judge in the world who won't throw me into a Secure Containment Facility, where I'll be lucky to see the sun for the rest of my sorry days. That's assuming my enemies don't find me first and save them the effort. There's no life for me down there. You know that.'

'*NINETEEN . . . EIGHTEEN . . . SEVEN-TEEN . . .*'

'Honey, you need help,' Easter said quietly as the timer counted down. 'You can get that down there, you can talk to people, understand why you do this, be a better person . . .'

'Help?' Honey cried. 'Who's going to help me?!'

'I will,' said Easter. 'I can't believe there isn't still some goodness in you somewhere. I know you, Honey. Not as Umbra. As Honey B. My friend. Let me help you.'

'Oh, I think you've helped me quite enough already,' spat Umbra, gesturing to her surroundings. 'You've taken everything from me. But at least I leave you knowing I'm taking something from you too.'

'What are you talking about?' Vi asked again. She had a horrible, horrible feeling about this.

'*SEVEN . . . SIX . . . FIVE . . .*'

As the counter reached its final few numbers, Umbra merely sauntered casually back to the space doors and opened her arms with a horrifying leer.

'Honey,' Easter pleaded again, a tremble in her voice. 'Please.'

'Goodbye, Easter Day,' Umbra spat as the timer ticked its final second and the space doors opened. 'Enjoy my parting gift, won't you?'

And with a maniacal scream, Umbra, Honey B, Vi's godmother, was sucked out into space.

Easter grabbed Vi into her with her good arm, shielding her daughter from the sight of her best friend's final seconds. Vi was surprised to feel a lone tear drop on to her cheek. But she knew what it signalled.

Umbra was dead.

The world was safe.

It was time to go home.

CHAPTER 17

'**D**arling, you're hurt!' George cried, racing to hug Easter as she and Vi returned to *Spinneret*.

'OUCH!' Easter cried at George's enthusiastic welcome.

'I'm so sorry,' George panted, looking like he might cry.

'I'm fine,' said Easter as Robert pulled out a first-aid kit to splint her arm. 'I've done worse, trust me. Let's just get out of here.'

'All systems prepared and ready,' said Russell from the control deck. Vi had noticed how comfortable he looked there. Perhaps Russell Sprout was destined for the stars one day. 'Ground control have prepared for us to land at a disused airfield near Ragnarok. They're ready when we are.'

'So she's really gone?' Robert asked Easter quietly as he and George tended to her arm.

Easter nodded. She looked . . . weird. Vi understood. Umbra might have been an evil super-villain. But for ten years, she'd been Easter's best friend. Her mum must be feeling really . . . weird.

Vi was just glad they were all safe.

Robert crouched down to Easter as he tied off the sling.

'Well done,' he said sincerely. 'You did a great job, Agent Lynx. I'd shake your hand, but . . .'

Easter laughed and punched Robert gently with her good arm.

'My pleasure,' she smiled. 'I just wish I'd done it right the first time.'

'Don't we all?' Robert smiled back and placed his hand over hers. Vi wasn't sure what he meant as her parents smiled happily at one another. But she wasn't convinced they were still talking about Umbra.

'Well, come on, everyone,' Easter said officiously as George kissed her softly on the head. 'Let's go home. I need a paracetamol.'

'I need something a lot stronger than a

paracetamol,' said Robert, strapping himself in. 'Where's your mother?'

'She's here,' came the quiet reply. Vi looked up at her nan standing in the airlock with Rod.

'About time too,' said Easter impatiently. 'Get a move on, Mum, we're not done yet. SPIDER still needs to blow this thing to smithereens and I don't want to be anywhere near it when they do.'

Vi looked at Nan. Something was wrong. Very wrong.

'I'm not coming,' Indy said simply.

'This is no time to be a stubborn mule, Mother,' Easter chided. 'Just get strapped in and we can get on our way.'

'I'm not coming,' Indy repeated. It took Easter a moment to realize what her mum was actually saying. But Vi understood straight away.

'What do you mean, you're not coming?' Easter said uncertainly. 'We have to get out of here, SPIDER is going to blow NIDUS up.'

'They can't,' Rod growled. 'Umbra tampered with the Doomsday switch. It won't work remotely. Someone has to manually activate it.'

Vi's guts knotted. So that's what Umbra had meant. That was her parting shot to them all. She was truly, truly evil. The full horror of what this meant hit Vi like a truck.

'So leave it,' said Vi desperately. 'Umbra's dead. Who else is going to come up here?'

'Someone,' said Indy. 'And given what we know this thing can do, we can't take that risk.'

'But if someone has to flick the switch, how are they going to get away?' Vi asked, although her sickening heart was already answering her own question.

Indy smiled at her granddaughter.

'They don't, my love,' she said gently. 'So it's like I said. I'm not coming.'

Vi felt her breath, her words, her heart and everything inside her shake. She looked over at Easter, who was clearly in the same place.

'You can't,' said Vi. 'You'll . . . you'll . . . you'll . . .'

'I'm afraid, my dear, that train has already left the station,' smiled Indy, coming over to her granddaughter. 'I told you, darling girl. Life is a ticking clock. And I'm on my final countdown anyway. Might as well put it to some use.'

'Mum, you can't do this,' said Easter tearfully. 'We need to get you home, get you to a hospital . . .'

'And spend what time I have left being poked and prodded like yesterday's dinner? No, thank you,' said Indy. 'You all have kids to raise. I've done my shift. And a bloomin' great job I did too, thank you very much. It's time to pass the baton. And it couldn't be in better hands.'

Vi waited for one of the adults to put up an argument, anything to change Nan's mind. But she could see they had nothing.

'You can't – I don't want – you shouldn't be alone,' said Easter weakly, the tears starting to flow.

'She won't be,' said Rod, taking Indy's hand and giving it a kiss. 'When I met your mother sixty years ago, I wanted to spend the rest of my life with her. And I have been privileged to have that chance. We're on this journey together. Every single step of the way. That's why I brought us all up here.'

'You did WHAT?' Robert and George said together. Rod's lips twisted into a naughty grin.

'You heard me,' he said. 'It was me who launched *Moonbreaker*. I knew those chumps down below wouldn't do half the job we would. And I was right. So now it's time to complete the mission.'

He looked at his beloved bride.

'Together,' he said gently, squeezing Indy's hand.

There was silence as they all contemplated the sacrifice Indy and Rod were about to make.

'Besides,' Rod added. 'The world was probably going to end tomorrow anyway. No big deal.'

Vi could just about make out Nan's smile through the tears. She knew now for sure she couldn't save her.

Because Independence Day didn't need saving.

'Come on, you lot,' said Indy, wiping her eyes. 'Let's get you out of here. No sense dilly-dallying about.'

'Indy,' said Robert, standing up and offering Indy his hand. 'I know we haven't always seen eye to eye. But please know that I think you are the bravest agent I have ever met. And I salute you, ma'am.'

Indy looked at the outstretched hand.

'Robert,' she said. 'I've had my doubts about you from the very start. And I was largely right. You were a lousy husband. But I believe you can be a great father.'

'Thank you,' said Robert, shaking her hand.

'Although you'll always be a complete idiot,' said Indy, shaking it back. Robert and Rod exchanged a salute as Indy took Russell and George into her arms.

'What a fine pair of Sprouts you are,' she laughed unevenly. 'You take good care of my girls, do you hear me?'

'I think you'll find they'll be taking care of us,' sniffed George.

Indy laughed.

'I think you're probably right,' she smiled. 'And as for you, young Russell. You go and grab that bright future by the sprouts, do you hear me?'

'I do,' said Russell tearfully. 'Thanks, Miss Indy. For everything.'

'Oh, pish,' said Indy, pushing them away. 'Now go and get ready. You need to get this bean tin safely back on the ground. Go and do . . . whatever it is you do.'

George put his arm around his son's shoulders and they made their way to the cockpit.

'Sprout?' Rod called after them.

'Yes,' they both said at once.

'Young Sprout, I mean,' Rod clarified. Russell wiped his eyes and headed over to Rod's scooter.

'Yes?' he asked quietly.

Rod went to his lapel and took off his *Commander* badge.

'If I'd have been blessed with a son,' he began. 'He wouldn't have been anything like you. He would have been bigger. Stronger. Wouldn't have needed glasses.'

'Thanks,' said Russell with a smile.

'But he wouldn't have been nearly as smart as you,' Rod continued. 'Lord knows I'm not. So I'm handing over command to you, Agent Sprout. I need you to see this ship home, get everyone back to Earth safely. This is your mission. Do you accept?'

'Aye-aye, Commander,' sniffed Russell as Rod pinned the badge on his jumper.

'Good lad,' said Rod, giving him a salute. 'Now, man your station.'

Russell paused for a moment before throwing himself at Rod for a huge hug.

'Yes, sir,' he said, then he straightened up again, turned and headed for the flight deck with George.

Vi watched with creeping horror as Indy took a sobbing Easter in her arms.

'Come on now,' Indy said to her daughter, rubbing her back as if she were a baby. 'We knew this day was coming.'

'I'm not ready!' cried Easter. 'I'm not ready to do this without you! I need my mum! I need you . . .'

'Pah!' spat Indy. 'You've not needed me for years! You're a brilliant woman, an incredible mum and a top agent. I've been in the passenger seat since I don't know when, my love. And this is my stop.'

Easter took a few steadying breaths and stood up straight.

'I love you, Mum,' she said. Vi could tell she was trying to hold it together for Indy. She didn't think she'd be able to do the same.

'I love you too, sweet girl,' said Indy, her voice starting to crack. 'Thank you for making me a mother. You have been by far my most successful mission.'

'And you've been by far the greatest mum,' Easter said, her hand trailing away from her mother's. She looked over to Vi.

'Come on, baby,' she smiled through her tears. 'It's time to say bye to Nan.'

Vi's feet stayed rooted to the ground. She couldn't do this.

'Get over here, you great plum,' said Indy, opening her arms for her granddaughter. 'We haven't got all day.'

Vi reluctantly forced her feet off the ground, and quickly found they were running towards her grandmother.

'There you go,' said Indy, wrapping her in one of her lavender hugs. Vi took in every feeling, sensation, smell and touch of her nan, determined to lock them in her heart and keep them there for ever.

'Now there's not many people in our profession who get to raise a child, let alone a grandchild,' Indy whispered. 'So you'd better promise you're going to be another one of them.'

Vi nodded into her nan. She couldn't imagine a day without Nan in it, let alone the rest of her life.

And more to the point, she really didn't want to.

'You've made me so proud, my darling Valentine,' said Nan. 'Keep fighting the good fights. And if you have half the happiness you've given me, you'll live a blessed life indeed.'

Vi clung on to her nan. She couldn't let go.

She stayed there for she didn't know how long, silently begging time to stop and freeze her in that moment. She wasn't ready. She wasn't ready for any of it.

'Time to go, baby girl,' she heard Easter say at last. She felt her mum's strong arm try to prise her gently away.

'No!' Vi cried. 'I don't want to go!'

'Agent Day!' Rod barked. 'You have received your mission! Do you really want your grandmother to see that snot-covered face? Now give us a smile! And that's an order!'

The ferocity of Rod's gruff commands shocked Vi out of her tears. He was right. This mission wasn't over. Not for her.

She looked up at Nan and gave her best attempt at a smile.

'Atta girl,' Nan winked back. 'Now get your little bum in that shuttle. Let's get this show on the road.'

The next however long was a blur to Vi. She heard Russell and George give each other various commands and she felt Robert strap her into her seat with a gentle kiss.

'Time to seal the doors,' said Russell gently.

'Everyone ready?'

Vi wanted to scream that, no, she wasn't ready, she'd never be ready. But she looked at her nan – her brave, beautiful and brilliant nan – and was determined to give her something better.

'Ready,' she said bravely, smiling and waving at her grandmother and her husband.

'Bye, Mum,' said Easter tearfully, accepting a hand-hold and a hankie from Robert.

'Bye, love,' said Indy, tears running down her smiling face. 'Pop the kettle on for me.'

Vi kept her eyes trained on her grandmother, smiling and waving right up until the second that the doors closed and took her from sight. For ever.

'Prepare for launch,' said George as evenly as he was able. 'We will be in orbit in three . . . two . . . one . . .'

Vi sensed her body being thrown around by the gravitational forces of *Spinneret*. But at that moment – and for the many that followed – she felt nothing.

'Everyone OK?' Robert asked quietly once they were safely launched into the darkness again. 'Is there . . . is there anything I can do?'

Vi shook her head.

'Well, I'm here if you need me,' Robert offered as Vi felt Easter's hand slip into hers.

They flew until NIDUS was a speck in the distance. Vi watched it get smaller and smaller. A sudden panic took hold of her – what if Nan and Rod changed their minds? What if the switch didn't work and they were stuck on NIDUS for ever? What if they were even now trying to contact *Spinneret* to tell them to come back and get them? What if—

The voices in her head were immediately and spectacularly silenced by a burning blaze of light illuminating the darkness. The speck that NIDUS had become was suddenly transformed into a shower of glittering stars. The whole vista before them lit up with the force of a thousand suns. It was strangely beautiful. It was horribly sad. But it was done. NIDUS and the Neurotrol were no more.

And neither was her nan.

Vi heard Easter, who had been watching with her, break down into heaving sobs. Vi floated over from her seat and went and curled herself in her mum's lap.

'Today we get to be sad,' she whispered. 'But soon we have to find our joy.'

'I know,' Easter cried. 'I just don't know how.'

'I do,' said Vi, looking at the stars gleaming on the horizon.

Because from deep within the depths of her pain, Vi knew that at least Nan had got something she'd always wanted.

Independence Day went out like a supernova.

CHAPTER 18

It was a quiet journey back towards the Earth's atmosphere. Tears were shed. Hands were held. Smiles were exchanged. Vi tried not to look at Nan's empty seat, feeling a lurching sensation in her stomach every time she did. She saw Easter looking too. Vi knew there were going to be a lot of empty seats where Nan should be sitting. It was going to take a long while to get used to them.

The blue beauty of the Earth grew bigger until it became the whole horizon. Vi could make out each of the continents – they were flying over Asia and Australasia when The Wolf's voice came crackling over the speaker.

'*Spinneret*? Do you copy, *Spinneret*?'

George went to pick it up, but then gestured to Russell.

'You get it,' he said. 'After all, you're the commander now.'

Russell smiled uncertainly before accepting the call.

'This is *Spinneret*, receiving you loud and clear,' he replied.

'You are clear for landing,' The Wolf confirmed. 'We've cleared the airbase runway for you. Commence your final preparations. You are coming home.'

Vi felt her heart leap at the words. Home. They were going home. Thank goodness.

'Just one thing,' The Wolf continued.

Vi felt her heart sink again. Of course there was just one thing. There was always just one thing.

'Our readings suggest that *Spinneret*'s insulation tiles sustained some damage during the battle with *Moonbreaker*,' The Wolf warned. 'It's not looking too serious, but we will monitor the situation.'

'Copy that,' said Russell. 'Dad – fire the RCS thrusters, we need the orbiter tail first. Then fire the OMS engines.'

'Aye-aye, Commander,' George smiled proudly. 'Consider it done.'

'Er, what was that about . . . the . . . thing?' Vi asked.

'The insulation tiles?' Russell replied distractedly. 'Because we're moving at approximately 28,000 kilometres per hour, the air molecules around us heat up to around 1,650 degrees Celsius. So we are covered with ceramic insulating materials to protect us from this friction.'

'Um, in English, please?'

'The spaceship is covered in stuff to stop us from cooking like a barbecued banana,' Robert explained. 'But some of it is damaged.'

'So what does that mean?' said Vi, her guts knotting up again.

'Probably nothing,' said George a little too casually.

'How probably?' Easter asked.

'Probably enough,' George reassured. 'The old girl's in good shape. We'll get her home safely.'

'Remember,' The Wolf continued. 'Ionization blackout means we will lose radio comms during re-entry. We'll do what we can from down here. But once you enter the Earth's atmosphere, you're on your own.'

'That'll make a change,' Robert muttered.

'Is there anything else you need us to do?' asked The Wolf.

George and Russell smiled at each other.

'I think we've got it, Agent Wolf,' Russell replied. 'See you on the ground.'

'You certainly will,' The Wolf confirmed. 'Good luck.'

As The Wolf signed off, Vi found herself feeling very alone. There was something comforting about having the team down there supporting them. Without it, they seemed somehow more vulnerable. More endangered. More scared.

'In a minute, we are going to slow everything down so that we effectively fall back to Earth,' George explained. 'Once we're in the main air of the Earth's atmosphere, we'll be able to fly *Spinneret* like she's an aeroplane.'

'Well, that's marvellous,' Robert added. 'Now who knows how to fly a plane?'

'I did an extra credit module on aviation,' Russell said, flicking buttons on the control panel. 'I've got a pretty good idea.'

Strangely, Vi found the notion of her twelve-year-old nearly-stepbrother flying them home in a damaged space shuttle a lot more comforting than she should. She trusted Russell completely. He was amazing. She really should tell him that.

At some point.

No rush.

'OK, everyone, we are entering the Earth's atmosphere in three, two, one . . .' Russell announced.

Vi felt *Spinneret* start to slow as the Earth's own gravity began to pull them home. It was nice to think that their own planet was pulling them towards it, like a welcoming hug.

Just so long as it didn't burn them to a crisp in the process.

'Burning RCS fuel,' George announced as *Spinneret* started to turn nose first again. 'Brilliantly done, Russ.'

'Thanks, Dad,' beamed Russell. 'I think that we're ready to—'

A sudden and very loud alarm flashing suggested that they were not, in fact, ready for whatever they were supposed to be ready for.

'What's that?' Easter asked tensely, holding on to her seat.

'It's the insulation panels,' said George calmly.

'We knew they weren't happy, it's just a precaution.'

'*WARNING – UNSUSTAINABLE TEM-PERATURE RISE DETECTED,*' *Spinneret* informed them. '*PREPARE EVACUATION PROTOCOL.*'

'That doesn't sound like a precaution to me,' Vi shouted over the various alarms now sounding. 'What's happening?'

'She's burning up,' said Russell plainly. 'She's not going to make it.'

'Well, I'd rather we did, old chap,' said Robert, sweat starting to form on his brow. 'What's the plan?'

'We need to disengage from the engine,' said Russell, furiously typing into the computer. 'We're close enough to parachute *Spinneret* down. If we jettison the engines here, we're still over the Pacific, they won't do any harm.'

'Russ, are you sure?' George said quietly. 'If we lose the engines, there is no way back.'

'I'm sure,' said Russell confidently. 'At this rate of acceleration, I calculate we have approximately seventeen seconds until the thrusters overheat – the whole ship will go up. You have to trust me on this.'

'I trust you on everything,' George said.

'I don't!' said Robert. 'He's a twelve-year-old boy! He can't be trusted to change his underwear! Although if this carries on, I might need to change mine . . .'

'Let him do his job, Dad,' Vi said, as calmly as she was able. 'Russell's the best. He knows what he's doing.'

Russell was too involved in saving their lives to acknowledge Vi's compliment. But she could tell from the proud hitch of his glasses that he'd heard her.

'Dad – you need to jettison the thrusters. Now,' he commanded.

'Jettisoning main thrusters,' George obeyed. 'Separating now.'

There was a huge clunk as the body of *Spinneret* separated from the engines that had delivered it to and from space. Vi watched them fall away from the shuttle. She hoped to goodness that her faith in Russell had been well placed, that he did indeed know what he was doing, that—

KER-BOOOOOOOOOM!

As the main thrusters exploded into a million pieces in the sky, Vi's answer came back extremely

300

quickly and really quite dramatically.

Russell Sprout had just saved all of their lives.

'Good call, old chap,' said Robert quietly, emerging from inside his own arms as the thrusters burnt up in the Earth's atmosphere. It didn't need pointing out that a few moments later, and that would have been all of them.

'We need to activate the emergency landing gear,' Russell ordered. 'We're not going to make it to the airbase. Dad, find us somewhere else to land – preferably on water.'

'Will do,' said George.

'Oh, no!' Russell suddenly exclaimed.

'Oh, no – what?' Vi asked.

'The emergency gear is password protected – I guess to stop anyone from accidentally deploying it,' Russell explained.

'Well, this is SPIDER's tin can. They must know it, surely?' Robert suggested.

'We're still in communication blackout,' Russell pointed out. 'We can't ask them. Come on – Rod designed this craft too, he will have created the password. Think, everyone – what would it be?'

There was a strange kind of frantic silence as

everyone racked their brains.

'Ragnarok?' Easter suggested.

'*PASSWORD INCORRECT*,' the *Spinneret* replied.

'Apocalypse?' George ventured.

'*PASSWORD INCORRECT.*'

'Tomorrow?' Robert guessed.

'*PASSWORD INCORRECT.*'

In her flurry of thoughts, Vi calmed her mind and let her nan's voice float into her head. Independence Day had been the best codebreaker of her – of any – generation. What would she do?

You don't just have to crack the code, she recalled Nan saying back at Gumfoot. *You have to crack the person.*

Rod created this passcode. What mattered to Rod more than anything else in this world?

She smiled as the answer lit up in her mind like a supernova.

'Lotus Flower,' she said confidently. 'Try Lotus Flower.'

There was a tense pause as everyone watched Russell input the passcode. They collectively held their breath. The ground was getting nearer. They needed that parachute . . .

'*PASSWORD   CORRECT*,'   *Spinneret*
responded. '*ACTIVATING   EMERGENCY
LANDING GEAR*.'

'You brilliant girl,' whispered Easter, a fresh tear
in her eye.

Vi smiled back. There might be some empty
seats where she would want Nan to be. But
there'd always be a space in her heart where Nan
would want to be. And that was going to help her
a lot.

'OK,' sighed Russell as the massive parachute
sprang out of the back of *Spinneret*, jolting them
on to their backs. 'That's one problem solved.
Dad, did you find us somewhere to land? Somewhere SPIDER can find us?'

'Oh, yes.' George gulped nervously. 'They
won't be able to miss us.'

There was an eerie quiet as the body of *Spinneret* whistled towards the Earth.

'So, what now?' Robert asked.

'Now – we wait,' said Russell, taking off his
headset and holding hands with his dad. 'And we
hope. There's nothing more we can do.'

Vi felt each of her parents slip a hand into hers,
Robert linking his other one with George, Easter

taking Russell's in hers. She looked proudly around. This was their family now. And whatever happened next, they were facing it together.

She closed her eyes and sat back in her seat. This was it. This was either the end of something incredible or the beginning of something even better. All she could do was wait.

Wait, and hope . . .

Reg took in grateful lungs of fresh air. All the commotion inside was getting a bit much. It reminded him of the third wedding of his second cousin Pauline – the one with the labradoodle and recurrent athlete's foot. Everyone running around shouting and screaming – it was just like when Pauline had left her hair straighteners (the nice ones she got from that fancy catalogue) on her labradoodle's bridesmaid's dress and set the sprinklers off right in the middle of her vows.

He looked out over Rod's vast grounds and felt a twinge that Rod wouldn't be coming back to enjoy them himself. Rod and Indy had become close to Reg during their time together at

Autumn Leaves and Reg felt an all-too-familiar sorrow at the loss of more friends. It was a sad beauty of his time of life that new friends never became old friends. Although perhaps you valued them all the more for the brief time you had them. Reg was entirely confident that Rod's home would be put to good use – maybe Ragnarok could become a nuclear bunker for retired agents? Rod would have liked that.

Reg wandered down the steps and into the grounds beyond. He headed for the vast lake that was at the heart of Rod's estate. He and Rod had talked about coming fishing here one day. Reg would miss that now. He'd miss a lot of things about Indy and Rod.

He took a seat by the lakeside. They didn't need him inside. If – as he desperately hoped it would be – it was good news on the way, it would find him here. If it were bad . . . Reg had lost too many loved ones to want to watch any more. He'd go and find bad news when he was ready.

It was a beautiful summer morning, the sun already casting its warmth across the ground. Today had a certain feel about it. When you'd woken up as many times as Reg had, you got a sense for these things. Today felt auspicious. Today felt exciting. Today felt—

KER-SPLASHSHSHSHSSHSHSHSHSHSH!

As a colossal space shuttle landed smack in the middle of Rod's lake, soaking Reg from head to toe, today felt rather wet.

Which, Reg smiled, also reminded him of Cousin Pauline's wedding.

CHAPTER 19

Vi had often wondered what her heaven would be like. She'd hoped for singing angels and golden harps and clouds. A gentle place for her to spend her eternal rest. With sweets. Lots of sweets.

But if she was indeed dead and this was indeed her heaven, it wasn't quite what she'd imagined.

'Vi?' she heard a male voice bark in her face. 'Vi?'

Vi wasn't quite alive enough to respond yet, so couldn't form the words.

A very cold splash of some very wet water soon brought her back to life.

'Eurgh!' she yelped, wiping the water from her face.

'What are you doing?' another voice floated up.

'Just . . . trying to help,' came the first.

She tried to open her eyes, but the light was too strong. She'd been in space for so long, she'd forgotten light. And it turned out that heaven was really bright. Must be all those golden harps . . .

'Take your time,' she heard the voice say more gently. 'It's OK, Vi. You're safe.'

Dad. That was her dad! So if she was in heaven, he'd come too. That was nice. Perhaps they'd meet Nan here?

'Nan?' she said groggily. 'Nan?'

'She must be concussed,' said a worried voice. 'She needs help.'

Vi smiled. Mum was here too. Good.

'Give her a minute,' said George. 'That was a big bang to the head.'

'Vi?' came Russell's voice. 'Wake up, Vi. We're here.'

Aw – the Sprouts had made it to her heaven as well. This was another family adventure. They were all together. Thank goodness for that.

She tried opening her eyes again, forcing them against the strength of the light. There they all were, her family, staring down at her, surrounded by halos of light. They were all angels!

Even her dad.

Wow.

'Can you get up?' Easter asked gently. 'Do you need help?'

'I'm fine,' said Vi, although she wasn't at all sure that she was. That light, it was so bright . . . but now she was getting used to it, she could start to make out her surroundings. She was still in *Spinneret*. But it was light outside. And there were . . . fish.

'Where are we?' she asked groggily.

'Smack in the middle of Rod's lake!' Robert chortled. 'It wasn't so much a crash landing as a splash landing!'

Vi groaned. She wasn't alive enough for her dad's cheesy jokes.

She allowed willing hands to help her to her feet. She looked out of the window at Ragnarok.

They were alive.

And they were home.

'We . . . we made it?' she asked in disbelief.

'Yes, we did,' said Easter, tearfully pulling Vi into her arms. 'We made it.'

'Agents! Agents!' came The Wolf's shout from outside. 'Are you OK in there? Requesting immediate situation report!'

The family smiled at one another.

'We're all fine,' Vi shouted out. 'Just get us out of here!'

A massive cheer erupted from outside the shuttle. Judging by her family's faces, Vi wasn't the only one who was surprised. There was clearly quite a crowd out there.

Either that, or Rod had some really weird fish. Both were possible.

'Stand by,' The Wolf commanded. 'We're opening the doors.'

Vi felt her mum squeeze her shoulders as the family gathered by the cargo door to go back out into the real world. The world that they had saved.

Together.

'Everyone ready?' George asked with a smile.

'Ready,' they all said as one, as the cargo door came away with a clunk and the outside world was finally let into *Spinneret*.

Still adjusting to the light, it took Vi a moment to comprehend the scene in front of her. Standing all around Rod's garden were crowds of people. Some she recognized – she waved to Reg, Auguste and Missy, who variously blew her kisses or gum bubbles back. Many she didn't – there were camera bulbs flashing and people screaming out their thanks and congratulations. All her senses were overwhelmed, not least her sense of smell as a familiar body threw itself at her dad.

'ROBBIE!' Siren gasped, planting an enormous kiss on Robert's lips.

'Hello, darling,' Robert crooned. 'It's so good to smell— To see you.'

'I swear, Robert Ford,' Siren exhaled. 'I'm never letting you out of my sight again. I want you to be like the hairy mole on my hip. Always by my side.'

'It's a promise,' Robert smiled as Siren picked Vi up and gave her a massive – and rather sweaty – hug.

Another figure ran out of the crowd, this one sweeping Russell off his feet.

'RUSSY!' his mother Genevieve sang out, making sure she turned to the cameras as she did. 'My son! My brilliant son! That's Genevieve with a G, by the way.'

'Hey, Mum,' said Russell, pulling himself away from the smothering of kisses showering his face. 'It's all good – I'm fine.'

'Oh, I know you are, sweetie,' said Genevieve, posing for the cameras once again. 'You're a hero!

You're everywhere! Everyone wants you! All the talk shows, all the magazines – we're . . . you're going to be famous! Now let's get you home.'

Genevieve pulled Russell's arm away and towards the cameras. But Russell wasn't budging.

'I am home,' he said. 'I'm with my family. That's where home is.'

Genevieve looked stumped. She turned nervously away from the screaming press.

'But, Russy, I am your family,' she said through clenched teeth. 'I'm your mummy. I want you home with me.'

'You are my mother,' said Russell. 'And I love you. But you can't pick and choose when you want me to be part of your family and when you don't. Families stick together, no matter what. I want you in my family, Mum. But you need to work a lot harder to be part of mine. And when you do, you'll be very welcome.'

Russell reached up to his mum and gave her a kiss on the cheek.

'See you soon,' he said, going back to his father's arms. 'You know where I am.'

Vi watched as Genevieve tried to form the words. But Russell had said them all. It was hard not to feel sorry even for Genevieve in that moment. But after a while she swallowed, nodded and some real tears glistened in her eyes.

'OK, then,' she said with a small smile. 'I hear you. Speak soon, Russy.'

Vi watched as Russell's mum turned away and disappeared back into the crowd.

'You OK?' Vi asked her nearly-stepbrother.

'Yeah,' said Russell, hitching up his glasses with a smile. 'You?'

'Yeah,' Vi grinned back, as The Wolf came to the front of the crowd.

'Agents,' he shouted, bringing everyone to a hush. 'The world owes you a debt of gratitude. You have given us the greatest of gifts – our freedom. We will never be able to repay what you have done. We thank you, sincerely, for your service.'

The crowd cheered enthusiastically and Vi felt her heart swell. They'd done it. The price had been high. But the world was safe.

'Before we celebrate – and celebrate we shall,' The Wolf declared. 'A moment's silence for our lost comrades. Independence Day and Rod Staff made the ultimate sacrifice so that no one else had to. Their selflessness and heroism will be re-membered for all time. They were the best of us, and we owe them everything. Agents Labyrinth and Redback, we salute you.'

At his call, the massed ranks of SPIDER, the Silver Service and even EVIL snapped to a salute. The crowd fell silent and Vi saw strangers from all walks of life pay their own private tributes to her grandmother and her husband. Some prayed according to their faith. Others stood quietly with their eyes closed and their hands folded. Many reached for the loved ones they had brought with them and stood with them in respectful gratitude. Her nan had brought all of these people together and, for that, Vi was incredibly proud.

She looked up to the sky where Indy had enjoyed her final adventure.

'I love you, Nan,' she whispered as she let her tears flow. 'Mission accomplished.'

CHAPTER 20

A year later, Vi was once again in a shocking bridesmaid's dress awaiting her parent's marriage. Saving the world, apparently, did not save you from a bride's appalling taste in dresses. But after a wild year, there was something lovely about being in a church packed to the brim with friends and family. There had been a time when Vi didn't know if she'd ever see any of them again. So being together felt like a blessing indeed.

'Valentine!' came a friendly shout down the aisle, accompanied by a cheerful bat-like squeak. 'I do not wish to objectify you in any way, nor suggest that you are identified by your appearance, but you look absolutely beautiful.'

'Dimitri! Nigel!' Vi exclaimed, accepting a hug from her old EVIL vampire friend – and a little wing-five from his pet bat. 'So good to see you – it's been ages!'

'We've been so busy with our new range of plant-based vampire food,' said Dimitri proudly. 'Remind me to send you some of our artichoke arteries.'

A large crash to her left alerted Vi to the arrival of Ted, who SPIDER had rescued from *Spiderling* six months previously.

'Hey, Ted!' Russell said happily, despite his awful bright blue pageboy suit. 'How are you doing?'

'Oh, still adjusting,' said Ted as he stepped heavily towards them. Vi smiled. After thirty years of living in a microgravity environment, Earth was proving a bit challenging for the astronaut.

'It's good to have you home,' Vi smiled. 'There's a seat over there if you want it?'

'Sure,' said Ted, jumping to float towards it, but ultimately crashing into a large pile of hymn books instead. Vi tried not to laugh as another old friend cannoned into her for a hug.

'TAMINA!' she squealed at her best friend from Rimmington Hall. 'Oh my days, it's so good to see you! I thought you were trekking in the rainforests?'

'Just back for a climate protest, then I'm off to monitor marine wildlife in Fiji,' squealed Tam. 'But when Russell mentioned the wedding, I thought, you know, maybe I should come and see you . . .'

Vi looked over to where Russell was blushing out of his skin. She should be offended that Tamina clearly wasn't there just to see her. But she wasn't.

'I'd better grab a seat – catch you at the reception?' Tamina gushed as Russell came over.

'You bet,' Vi winked. 'Good to see you.'

'You too, hero,' Tam winked back. 'Always knew you'd save the world one of these days.'

'You keep saving it too,' smiled Vi as two unfamiliar guests caught her eye, jostling one another in the second pew back.

'Who are they?' Vi asked Russell out the side of her mouth. 'Are they your family?'

'Never seen them before,' Russell whispered back. 'But they haven't stopped arguing since they got here.'

'I'm telling you, this is the right place,' huffed the brown-haired white girl. She was probably only a few years older than Vi, but something about her seemed very much older.

'And I'm telling you, you are a moron,' the blond-haired white boy shot back, mischief sparkling in his blue eyes. 'This is just like when Dad had to take you to hospital before the Brysmore Summer Concert.'

'How was I to know that "break a leg" meant good luck,' the girl shot back. 'It's not my fault that mortal languages are so suboptimal. And it was only a sprain.'

'Er, can I help you?' Vi asked as the boy flicked the girl's ear.

'Thank you, kind stranger,' the girl replied. 'We are just awaiting the arrival of our friend. He's getting married today. Again. Do you know the bride, Tracey?'

'Stacey,' the boy interrupted. 'It was Tracey last month.'

'No, it's Tracey,' the girl insisted. 'I clearly remember her face.'

'That's because they are twins,' the boy pointed out impishly.

'Oh, Zeus,' the girl sighed, getting to her feet. 'Well, if we are in the wrong place, it's all your fault.'

'How do you figure that?' the boy said. 'Look, just shout out for the wedding organizer, they'll be able to help.'

'Fine,' sighed the girl. 'What's their name?'

'I. Nead-Apu,' said the boy with a wicked twinkle. 'But make sure you shout it really loud. They're a little hard of hearing.'

'It's always down to me, isn't it?' said the girl, turning around to face the congregation. 'I just hope this I. Nead-Apu character is more professional than the Seymour Bumms you told me to find at the last wedding. They weren't even there, anyway . . .'

Vi reached over to stop the girl, just as she took a big breath to shout out across the church.

'Um . . . I think you've got the wrong venue,' she whispered. 'This is my family's wedding. And we're about to start, so . . .'

'My vast apologies,' said the girl sincerely. 'You'll have to forgive my idiotic companion. I hope you have a highly optimal day. So sorry for interrupting your celebrations.'

'Don't worry about it,' Vi smiled as they jostled out of the pew.

'I just don't know what you'd do without me,

Elliot Hooper,' she heard the girl huff as they walked out of the church. 'First, I save the world, then I save you . . .'

'You didn't save the world! *I* saved the world!' the boy argued.

'You couldn't save your pocket money,' the girl scoffed. Who were these two?

'Virgo. Go and boil your head,' the boy shot back as they and their voices drifted out of the church.

Vi smiled.

Save the world. Bless them. As if.

She looked to the now empty pew. That's where Nan would have been sitting, her hair dyed celebratory pink. She smiled and blew a kiss to the empty space. She'd learnt to do that over the past year. It really helped. Nan and Rod would be watching from somewhere. Vi believed they always were.

A commotion broke out at the back of the church as her mother and George burst through the doors.

'You're late!' Vi hissed to Easter and George as they hurtled down the aisle. 'You two and weddings!'

'I'm so sorry,' said Easter, handing George the baby girl they had welcomed to the family three months earlier. 'Your sister is going for some kind of world nappy-filling record – she's like a Mr Whippy machine.'

Vi and Russell waved to the baby sister they now shared. She was super-cute – if smellier than Siren. Vi could accept that she had a sister called Christmas. But Christmas Day-Sprout? Only in *her* family.

'Quick – we need to get in place,' said Vi as the groom took his position.

'Good luck,' George whispered as he sat down next to Easter. Since they'd got back to Earth, Mum and George had given up on the idea of getting married, for everyone's safety. It was probably a wise decision.

Vi grinned as George took out his tinfoil matchbox with upgraded cocktail umbrella. George had been using it regularly ever since they returned to Earth. And Fido wouldn't want to miss this.

'You ready?' Vi said to the groom.

'As I'll ever be,' Robert replied nervously as a low saxophone started playing the wedding march from the back of the church.

All eyes turned to the top of the aisle, where the bride looked radiant in a white PVC gown – although the reaction was less enchanting as she walked down the aisle, the quiet sounds of gagging filling the church as Siren progressed towards her new husband.

'You look . . . exceptional,' said Robert as his bride took her place next to him.

'I took worming tablets especially,' said Siren with a wink. 'Let's do this thing.'

They both turned to the vicar.

'Dearly beloved,' the vicar began. 'We are gathered here today to celebrate . . . er, David? Do you mind?'

Dave took the saxophone out of his mouth. But for once, he didn't look cool about it.

'This is an absolute OUTRAGE!' he cried in a very high, very posh voice, yanking off his hat and glasses. 'I'm sick and tired of being treated like some two-bit busker! If I'm good enough for the Berlin Philharmonic, I'm good enough for you! You are philistines! And I QUIT!'

And with that, the saxophonist turned on his heel and dramatically stormed out of the church.

'Wow. Dave. Chill,' said Robert with a wink at his daughter.

Vi groaned. Siren had better get used to a whole new soundtrack – her dad's cheesy jokes.

'Shall we?' Robert asked the vicar.

'Yes . . . so, as I was saying,' the vicar flustered, 'we are gathered here today to celebrate the marriage of—'

An almighty blast exploded at the back of the church.

'SIR CHARGE! SIREN! Sorry to crash the wedding, but I have an objection! A really unlawful objection!'

The intruder fired a massive shot from her gigantic bazooka, shooting a stone angel off the organ.

'Apoco-Lips!' Siren hissed, reaching for the shotgun she'd still somehow managed to conceal in her wedding dress. 'What are you doing here?'

'Settling an old score!' the super-villain replied. 'I've got a nuclear rocket pointing straight at Big Ben! I want a billion dollars or I blow London sky-high! And nothing and no one can stop me!'

Vi looked at her dad, who looked at Siren, who looked at Russell, who looked at George, who looked at Easter. They all smiled.

'You reckon?' Vi said, ripping off her brides-maid's dress to reveal her black agent all-in-one underneath.

Easter handed baby Christmas to George and pulled a bottle out of the nappy bag.

'She'll need a nap at three and don't forget to burp her after her lunchtime bottle – you know how gassy she gets,' she said, kissing George on the head. 'I'll be home for dinner.'

'Love you, sweetie,' said George, bobbing Christmas up and down on his lap. 'Don't work too hard.'

'APOCO-LIPS!' said Easter, yanking the teat out with her teeth. 'You messed with the wrong family. You haven't got the bottle!'

And with that, Easter lobbed the bottle down the aisle, which promptly exploded at the super-villain's feet. Siren, Robert and Easter all sprang into action, charging down the aisle to take down their enemy.

Vi and Russell grinned at one another.

'You ready?' Russell asked, offering his hand.

'Born ready,' Vi replied, taking it in hers. 'Let's go and kick some butt!'

And as Valentine Day sprinted down the aisle towards her next mission, she threw her head back and laughed.

Life with her family was never going to be straightforward.

But it was sure as heck always going to be an adventure.

MISSION ACCOMPLISHED

END-OF-MISSION REPORT

I must begin the final words of thanks for this series with an apology – to anyone who knows anything about space. While I have immeasurably enjoyed my research for this novel (space toilet hoovers – who knew?!), it is the privilege of the author to mould the facts around their story, a liberty I have taken extensively in this book. As with everything I write, while I hope my words have their feet on the ground, they also have their head in the clouds and as such – frankly I've made loads of stuff up. If you are interested in space and space travel, nasa.gov has a galaxy of actual information that will tell you the truth rather than spin you a yarn.

I started this series just as the real world faced the greatest threat I've known in my lifetime – I end it as we hopefully start to emerge into a brighter future. It has been a time to reflect a great deal on who and what matters in this little life, and I feel more grateful than ever to have been given the opportunity to spend my days doing something I utterly love. That gift was given to me by all at Chicken House and so, as ever, my thanks must go to that galaxy of stars, especially my North Star, Rachel Leyshon, who always helps to chart my course and tries to save me from too many black holes. I am indebted too to Laura Myers, who has now made seven books much better than they ever would have been without her. If anyone can sort this universe out, it is Laura – and she'll make sure all the apostrophes are in the right place too.

My agent Veronique Baxter continues to pilot my shuttle with her steady hand, no matter what ridiculous stargazing I dream up, and I would drift in a hopeless orbit without her. Jez Tuya, Helen Crawford-White and Steve Wells have made this series look stellar and I'm so grateful for their time and artistry. Thank you also to Jenny and Adamma for ensuring all the right words go in all the right places. I must learn to do that myself one of these days.

This book is dedicated to my dad, Andrew Evans, who introduced me to James Bond, probably much earlier than he should have. We've watched them all together, and when I needed to dream up an idea for a new series, it was those Sunday afternoons on the sofa that inspired this one. You're more Johnny English than James Bond, Dad — but I loves ya and it's been a pleasure to serve with you. I will forever be your 'M'.

It's always a joy when life imitates art — and Easter and George's efforts to get married over the past few years have had nothing on mine. But Never Say Never (Again), Johnny B — our day will come. I love you and we have all the time in the world. To Ian — thank you for being the best friend and co-pilot imaginable as we raise our junior cadets. I'm still Commander, just to be clear. And to Agents Z, L and D — I love you with my everything. Thank you for bringing me joy every single day, you little superstars. And if you thought I was like Easter when you were younger — just wait now you're teenagers.

As *Who Let the Gods Out?* did before it, this series has spanned a lot of new chapters in my own story, ones that I never planned but have made my tale stronger for their presence. I think the clearest lesson I have learnt over these strangest of years is the vital value of kindness.

The pandemic has often demonstrated the very best of humanity's capacity to be kind, and has made me work harder to put more of it into the world myself. I hope that you, my brilliant readers, will strive to do the same. For if we all commit to being a little kinder every day, the Umbras of this world don't stand a chance.

Thank you, thank you, thank you again for coming on this journey with me. I have so many more exciting adventures on and off the page coming your way over the next few years. I hope so much to have your company for the ride.

Love, and other things that reach the stars,

Maz

xxx